It's Grim Up North
A Zombie Tale

Copyright © 2017 Sean Wilkinson

All rights reserved

No parts of this publication may be reproduced, stored in a retrieval system, or transmitted in any form or by means, electronic, mechanical, photocopying, recording or otherwise, without the prior written permission of the copyright owner.

This book is sold subject to the condition that it shall not, by way of trade or otherwise, be lent, resold, hired out, or otherwise circulated without the publisher's prior consent in any form of binding or cover other than that in which it is published and without a similar condition including this condition being imposed on the subsequent purchaser. Under no circumstances may any part of this book be photocopied for resale.

This book is a work of fiction. Any similarity between characters and situations within its pages and places and persons, living or dead, is unintentional and coincidental.

Foreword

First of all I'd like to thank you all for taking the time to read the book and spending your hard earned money to do so.

I'd never had any plans of ever writing to be honest. There was absolutely no planning involved, no story board or plot design. It just sort of happened one day and started spilling out of my head.

In the beginning it was just something to do to pass the time at work. Then it became rather enjoyable. I'd never planned on letting anyone else actually read it.

I'll be honest, it's never going to be a best seller but the friends that read the rough draft really enjoyed it. Apparently. I just hope they weren't blowing smoke up my arse.

Like the narrator of the book I've always had a morbid fascination with anything apocalypse related. I think everyone does in some way. Having the revelations drummed into us all from birth. Gods wrath has always been around the corner, threatening to smite the sinners and non-believers.

The zombie thing is a passion I've had since I can remember. Unlike supernatural horror, the walking dead are predictable. I like that about them.

A very big thank you to my guinea pigs that read the rough draft. Kevin, Richard Cheesman, Julie Butler and family, Bryan Haddock, LL, Uncle John, Auntie Paula, my Mammy and Bob.

Thank you for giving me the courage to share the book and take this big step.

Also, a big thank you to Jo Kemp for proof reading for me. It's much appreciated.

Enjoy!

It's Grim Up North!
A Zombie Tale

Chapter 1 – The 'hero'

I always knew it would happen. The culling of mankind; the apocalypse!

Never in my wildest dreams did I think the cause of it would be zombies. Yep, fuckin zombies. I'll admit, I may have fantasised on numerous occasions that it would be the cause, but never did I think it could actually happen.

Don't get me wrong. I'm not a sicko or some religious nut praying for the rapture. Well, maybe a little, but twenty years of cannabis abuse, video games and hundreds of zombie books and films can do that to a person.

Let me begin by telling you a little about myself, before you start making judgements. My name is Carter. That's not my real name. It's my stage name. I chose it in homage to one of my favourite films and I thought it would be harder for the tax man to find me with this pseudonym. I'm a 'professional' singer on the local club scene in the northeast of England. Sounds cool? Not really.

When I say club scene I don't mean night clubs filled with young scantily clad twenty somethings drinking £10 cocktails, I mean social clubs. Yes, the working man's bingo emporiums filled with old-aged pensioners, cheap ale and urine-stained carpets. Not so glamorous now!

I left school at sixteen and fell into the job when my father told me I should give it ago after he'd heard me singing in the bath one night. My father had experience in this vocation, having been a singer himself, and had witnessed the clubs in their heyday, when they'd been the sole source of weekend entertainment for the working man. The good old days when punters would queue up early in order to get a good seat to watch 'the turn', shout 'house' and make a sizeable dent in their weekly wage packet. I got into the scene as it was starting to wind down and was lucky to have more than twenty in the audience on most nights. The reason for this was simply that the men in charge had refused to move with the times. Their members were literally dying off and weren't being replaced.

The youth of today refused to be told to sit quietly during the religious ritual of the bingo, which was tediously played for the majority of the night. To be honest, there was never any chance in hell of me ever spending a night off in any of the places I've performed. I didn't blame the young for taking a wide berth of those archaic buildings from a forgotten time.

So, to cut a long story short, twenty-five years later, after numerous rock bands and cabaret work, not to mention the uncountable relationships and drug use, I find myself here. Writing down my harrowing account of the end of days.

As I mentioned earlier, I had secretly fantasised about what I would do in the event of a zombie apocalypse. This was probably down to the side effects of paranoia that come with prolonged chemical intake. Who knows? Everywhere I went I found myself weighing up my surroundings and the thousands of different scenarios that could play out because of the decisions I made. Escape routes, defensible positions, usable weapons, how to get home, which of the zombie grannies to kill first, etc.

Now I know this sounds strange, but I really enjoyed playing these survival games in my head and it also got me through endless hours of bingo and meat draw raffles.

I'd been this way since I was young. Paranoid about an apocalypse, that is. I was around six years old when the survival bug bit me. I remember it like it was yesterday. I was playing with my Lego in front of the television while my parents watched the nightly news. I can remember hearing the words 'Cold War' and looking up at the screen. On it, was a black and white film of what looked to be some sort of warship. Then the screen suddenly went white. When the camera focused in again, the ship had been replaced by a gigantic mushroom cloud.

I innocently turned to my parents and asked, 'What the fuck was that?' After my ear had stopped burning from the clip I received, they nonchalantly told me the Russians didn't like us and could bomb us at any moment. WTF?

Little did they realise what effect this had on my emotional and mental wellbeing. For years after this I would time myself with a stopwatch to gauge how long it took to run home from school, because one of the bigger boys in the neighbourhood had told me that we'd most definitely get a four-minute warning of our imminent destruction. The school was over a mile away and no matter how much I watched *Chariots of Fire*, I soon realised I was never going to match Mr Bannister and get home before I was atomised. Still, the redundant coal shed in our back garden was repurposed as my own personal bunker, knowing full well that there wasn't any room for my parents. That'll teach them for being so flippant about the ruskies. And for clipping my fuckin lugs.

I equipped the bunker with assorted bags of crisps, an old duvet, a torch, a couple of *Beanos* to read and a change of underpants. I was ready for the nuclear holocaust! Little did I know that even if I did survive the initial blast, the meagre walls of the coal shed would fail to keep out the radiation from the resulting fallout. I'd most likely die a slow and painful death, poisoned, alone with only the Bash Street Kids to keep me company.

When communist Russia fell and the iron curtain came down my worries abated. Even more so when puberty kicked in. My fallout shelter was again repurposed and used as a place to hide my nudey magazines and also a secluded place to go and 'study' them. A lot.

But it didn't take long for my worries to resurface with a vengeance. Especially when sweet Mary Jane was introduced to me in my late teens and multiplied my paranoia ten- fold. So much so that at the turn of the century I started hoarding bottled water and dried food in my shed, much to the amusement of my friends and family. The crisis at the time was the apparently unavoidable resetting of all computers over a certain age. Some of these computers supposedly still controlled some very important aspects of the everyday running of the world in general. Bank computers, air traffic control towers, power grids, to name but a few, were due to reset and bring the world into chaos. This alone was terrifying, but when some egghead added that most of the world's nuclear devices could go pop, my paranoia went through the roof.

    Adding to my acute mental problems were the prophetic writings or 'quatrains' of a certain sixteenth-century French dude.

> The millennium bug came and went. Nostradamus was full of shit.

    The ridicule I received from my nearest and dearest would have probably made lesser men forget all about the survival silliness. It didn't. It made me worse. What if something like that could happen? The world is proper fucked up after all.

The country had had a little taster of this during the fuel crisis in the year following the millennium bug. For just over a week in September of that year the nation came to a virtual standstill as protesters blocked the crucial flow of fuel. The protesters, consisting mainly of farmers and HGV drivers, were aggrieved at the sudden rise in the price of fuel. They promptly blockaded all oil refineries in the country.

Within twenty-four hours, petrol stations started running dry as the demonstrations began to bite and motorists launched in to panic buying, which also spread to the supermarkets, with the public rushing to stock up on essential items.

The protests ended almost as quickly as they began, but not before the army had been put on standby to transport supplies, mail deliveries had been hit and the Government had staged crisis talks.

And so, I immersed myself in all things survival and being a 'professional' singer – only really working at weekends, I had ample spare time through the week to concentrate on my new addiction. I even attended a few extreme survival courses. I was like a sponge.

Eventually the paranoia started to wain when I fell out of love with Mary Jane and I practised my new skills for fun, never thinking I'd actually have to use them. I'd solo hike to remote woodland and mountains and spend days testing myself in fire building, water purification, shelter construction, tracking, trapping and skinning, fishing, first aid, hiking and countless other techniques for staying alive.

The fixation with zombies was instilled in me at an early age too. Before the popularity that was brought on by the multitude of zombie TV series and big-budget movies, I had been an avid fan. Bootleg copies of George's cult films were difficult to come by at the tender age of ten, but *Dawn*, *Day* and *Night of the Dead* became my nightly viewing for years. While my parents sat downstairs assuming their little angel was sleeping, I was upstairs terribly scarring my innocent mind. I went on to consume anything zombie. Books were next, the adventure kind, where at the end of each chapter, the reader would be given a choice of which way the story could go. One of the choices would be correct the other always ended in a gruesome death. I had an uncanny knack for this and never chose the wrong option. Maybe that's why I'm still alive. Unbeknown to me I'd been training myself all those years ago.

Technology advanced and brought us one of the most important inventions of the twentieth century. That's right. The PlayStation! No longer did the stoner just veg out in front of the TV. They went on adventures instead. Raiding tombs, driving at high speed and killing the Nazis became the new norm. Then came the eagerly awaited release of the first real zombie game. The umbrella corporation unleashed the t-virus onto the world and I was the only one who could save it. And save it I did, lots. What can I say? I only worked three nights a week. The rest of the time I spent in a purple haze, sitting on the floor in front of the TV, fucking shit up.

So, here I am. A single, balding, forty-something musician, putting pen to paper to tell my story about the zombie Armageddon.

At the moment, I'm tucked away in my 'lair', safe, for the time being, from the reach of a billion claws and teeth. The events that brought me here are unbelievable, terrifying and heartbreaking, but have made me stronger and more self-aware than I have ever been in my life. The lessons I learned in the early days taught me to have faith in my intuition and knowledge. And never to give up, no matter what dire situation I'm in. Never fucking give up!

Chapter 2 – The end

It started late one balmy summer night in June. For some reason, maybe because of the heat through the day, I couldn't sleep. But I needed desperately to get some shut eye. My alarm was set for 6am so I could get to the gym for 6:30am. Another addiction of mine since I turned forty. #midlifecrisis

So, while waiting for the warm milk I'd drunk to kick in, I turned on the TV and chose the news channel to cure my insomnia.

Usually at that time of night there would be some financial boffin on air, explaining the pros and cons of the upcoming Brexit referendum. Britain was voting whether or not to stay within the European Union. For some reason, the prime minister had thought it a good idea to let the country vote for something they didn't really understand. The debate had been hijacked by the far right nationalist party, who turned it into a hate campaign pointed towards immigrants and refugees. We'd been force-fed lies and propaganda for months and it was all starting to become tiresome.

The perfect subject to get me off to sleep.

However, what I was about to witness would have me wishing it had been financial jargon and Brexit shit I was watching.

As soon as the TV came on, shouting and screaming filled the room, amplified by the hi-fi speakers I'd linked up to the TV. Scrambling for the remote I lowered the volume and stood aghast at what my eyes were witnessing.

At first it looked like any other riot, like the ones we'd had a few years earlier in London, when anyone under the age of twenty took to the streets in 'protest' at a young black man being assaulted and killed by the police. I say protest in inverted comas because the majority of the rioters had not come to voice their concerns about the mistreatment of the young man. They'd come to loot and rampage and generally just fuck the place up. Most of it planned and encouraged on social media, it soon snowballed out of control and embarrassingly demonstrated to the world the worst aspects of popular culture and, in essence, human nature.

The events I was now viewing, on closer inspection, were nothing like that. No hundred-yard stand-off with the police. No projectiles were being thrown. No Molotov cocktails. No one running off with electrical appliances. Just complete and utter chaos.

The riot police stood aligned, pushing against a surge of around one hundred crazed people of all ages, their five-foot riot shields forming a solid wall.

The news anchor covering the proceedings was on the verge of panic as she stood behind the police line commentating on the 'riot'. She was a pretty blonde girl in her late thirties. Although with the stress lines on her face and the large bags under her eyes it was hard to judge – she may have been younger. She was probably only used to reporting the weather at this time of the night, instead of the frightening things that were happening in front of her.

She turned towards the camera and proceeded to explain the situation with a noticeable shake in her voice. 'As you can see behind me, an unexplained riot has broken out at the entrance of Stanstead airport. Reports are claiming that flight LM4470 from Saudi Arabia emergency landed after the pilot reported a possible terrorist encounter on the aircraft. Anti-terrorist specialists stormed the plane shortly after the aircraft taxied from the runway. They were then apparently attacked and overrun by the passengers on the flight.

All incoming flights have been diverted until this threat has been neutralised.'

She added, 'Sources have informed us that the passengers of LM4470 have disembarked after overpowering the military personnel and have proceeded to attack numerous other travellers and staff throughout the airport. There have also been unconfirmed reports of victims of the passengers of LM4470, including the anti-terrorist officers, joining the ranks of the rioters.'

In the blink of an eye, the cameraman's attention turned towards the right flank of the police line to where a policeman was savagely dragged into the fray. A blood-curdling scream I thought couldn't have possibly come from a human being pierced the night.

Give the cameraman his due. He never took the camera from the very graphic demise of the policeman. The rioters fell on him like a pack of wolves on a rabbit. They literally tore him to pieces. Not only that, they raised the pieces to their mouths and started feasting.

FUCKIN' HELL!

The wall of shields collapsed in seconds when the other police witnessed this and the line fell while Her Majesty's finest turned and fled in abject terror. Screams echoed around my living room as a few foolishly brave officers who didn't flee were brought down and and slaughtered in the same way as the first policeman.

At this point the camera fell to the ground and went black. I'll never know what happened to the news reporter or the cameraman, but by the way things were going I didn't hold out much hope for them.

My first thought was, 'Fucking zombies!' I'm not going to lie, I did have to suppress the corners of my mouth from rising skyward at first, but then the slaughter I'd just witnessed and enormity of it all hit me like a ton of bricks. This must be a joke. I turned to another news station. Same thing, different airport. What? Different airport? I sat down.

This report was coming from Manchester. More or less the exact same scene filled my screen. A ticker tape scrolled along the bottom reporting riots at three other airports around the country.

Now at a time like this, your first thought is for your loved ones. I was lucky in a way that I had none. Well, not lucky, but you know what I mean. I did have an ex who lived in the next town over but that had ended messily due to me being a dick and subsequently left me utterly heartbroken. She'd moved on, and met a young, good looking fitness instructor. Yep, a fucking fitness instructor. I know how clichéd that sounds. But it was true, and to be honest, if she was happy, I was happy for her. I loved her and always would but he was a fuckin twat. I'm not bitter.

So, it was me, myself and I. Not one for jumping to conclusions, I decided to confirm what was going on before I set off into the wilderness with my bugout bag, started eating woodlouse from under fallen trees and wiping my arse on dock leaves. It'd be just my luck to be found twenty years from now like a Japanese soldier who hadn't known the war was over. I needed to know what was going on without any bias from the TV. That meant Facebook.

Facebook, as usual, was full of shit. Videos of kittens, racist posts about immigrants and photos of people's dinner. I really didn't know why I still had that stupid app.

The thing did more damage than good. Usually, when I'd had a few too many, it became a platform to vent my frustrations, which often included abuse thrown at the ex and Mr fucking six-pack man. I'm really not bitter!

There were a few posts, however, relating to the news broadcast I had recently viewed. WTF prevalent throughout the said posts. OMG was there too. Goosebumps erupted all over my body when one particular post from a friend of mine from Islington, London wrote, 'What the fuck is going on? Sirens are blaring all over the fucking place.' Henry Hutton-Wingate was his name. Not his real name I might add. Like me he had stage name. His real name was Davey Holly. I met him when we were both the tender age of nineteen. We shared a guitarist and a bass player. I had them at weekends and he had them midweek. I would get them to play cover songs to the grannies and he'd get them to play his own material to the jet set of the Newcastle music scene. We never really got on at first. This was mainly an alpha male thing we'd had between us, but over the years our friendship grew stronger.

He'd moved down to London in his mid-twenties to become an actor, hence the double-barrelled name change. He'd done quite well actually, starting off in TV ads, then the soaps and finally ending up on the West End. Being able to sing as well as act progressed his career and made him a household name. Whoop de fuckin doo.

I wasn't jealous at all.

The post he'd written on Facebook was only a few minutes old, so I wrote him a quick reply telling him to check the news and lock the doors. He replied with, 'Are you pissed?'

Now please don't go thinking that I'm well known for being a party animal. I admit I used to be but have been drug free for a number of years and only ever drink on very special occasions or when I feel the need to visit Facebook to have a swipe at the happy fucking couple. I'm not bloody bitter!

A few minutes later my friend messaged me back. 'Mate, WTF, fucking zombies!!! this can't be real. Are you playing games?'

I am also known to have been a bit of a joker in my time, but not once have I ever employed over a hundred people, police officers, a special effects makeup team and a computer whizz kid to hack into the news channels all in the aid of a gag. I must admit, if I had the money and the imagination to do such a thing I probably would. But I didn't.

> I replied to him and told him to double check the doors and to keep in touch.

I focused on the TV again and realised that the news wasn't on anymore. Just the news channel's logo and a statement saying they were experiencing technical problems. Fucking technical problems? Yeah, your cameraman and news anchor have just been fucking eaten mate. There's nothing technical about that.

As I flicked through the channels I found that they were showing the same message. I thought, 'This must be serious if the infomercials and the roulette shows have ceased to function.'

I checked the internet. It was off. Mobile phone signal. Gone. Radio. Nada. There was a message flashing from my Facebook friend. He must have sent it before the net went down. It read. 'Fuck me mate. I think those people are in my street. They're banging on doors and smashing windows. Shit, there's someone coming down my path.'

The message ended there. Even though he'd turned into a southern softie and took to wearing a coat in winter, I really hoped he'd be ok.

Suddenly my brain kicked in to gear. Was this it? Was it really happening? The final chapter in the story of humanity? The end result? Armafuckingeddon?

Chapter 3 – The 'keep'

If it was the end, I had to secure the house before anything else.

At that moment in time I was living in a small rented house on a very nice estate in a place called Cramlington in Northumberland. I'd moved there when I separated from the ex. I liked it. It was close to the A1 motorway and the Tyne Tunnel, it had a nice local pub, lots of shops, a cinema and was close to the gym. All I needed.

The estate had two ways into it by road and had lots of wide cycle paths if the roads became congested and I needed to get the fuck out of dodge!

The main weakness of the lovely two-bedroom house were the front door and the living room bay window. I quickly went outside and positioned my van, which was around fifteen feet long and seven feet high, against said door and window with the side door of the van in line with the front door of the house. I was surprised none of the neighbours came out while I performed a thirty-two-point turn on the unkempt front lawn, which was absolutely ruined now anyway with divots and tyre marks all over it. Sorry mister landlord. Just take it out of my bond!

There was about a six-inch gap between the house and the van. Just enough for the van door to pop out and slide open. The back garden was enclosed by a very sturdy wall/fence combo and could only be accessed through the garage or the kitchen.

That done, I went and filled the bath with water. One of the 'rules of three' for survival. I'd learned this on one of my survival courses: three minutes without air or in zero degree Celsius water, three hours without shelter, three days without water and three weeks without food.

I had plenty of air and my shelter was sorted – the tub full of water was another check on the 'rules of three'. I did have a lot of bottled water stored in the garage but it's best to have something and not need it rather than need something and not have it.

While the bath was running I quickly entered the garage through the garden and dragged the mountain of camping equipment I'd acquired over the years in to the house.

Not forgetting my bugout bag.

I imagine you're wondering exactly what a bugout bag is. It's a prepper thing. I'd had it hanging in the garage for around fifteen years and would replenish its perishable contents every six months or so. It contained everything you needed to survive in the wilderness for around two weeks.

It had: a lightweight sleeping bag, a waterproof bivi bag that enshrouds the sleeping bag, a waterproof tarp, fire-lighting kit with various tinder and lighters, water purification pump, a small survival kit (with fishing hooks and line, water purification tablets, flint and steel), compass, torch, candles, a solar battery charger, maps of the surrounding area for a hundred miles in every direction, first-aid kit, food for two weeks, two litres of water in a camelback, a wind-up radio, survival knife, multi-tool, a hundred metres of paracord, changes of clothes, toilet roll, a fifteen-inch bolo machete and a pistol-type crossbow which I'd bought for shits and giggles.

I opened the front door and the van door and loaded it with some of the larger camping equipment I'd chosen to take if I needed to bug out in the van by road. The fiveman tent went in with the inflatable bed, gas lamp, chairs, four-season sleeping bag and about a week's supply of food and water. I left the bugout bag on the settee in the living room in case I needed to hightail it on foot.

As I closed the door, I listened to the birds singing and watched the sun begin to rise in a terrifically beautiful clear sky but also on a very different world.

Chapter 4 – The decision

While listening to the birds' dawn chorus I suddenly realised that I could hear the faint sounds of sirens in the distance. It had been over four hours since I first saw the news report. The shambling fuckers couldn't have made it this far north already, could they? I slapped my hand to my forehead Oliver Hardy style. Newcastle airport! It was only a fifteen minute drive from my house. The sirens could well have been unrelated to the events that were occurring around the country, but I wasn't going to take any chances.

It was time for a decision to be made. Do I jump in the van and literally head for the hills?

Northumberland is host to a range of hills called the Cheviots. Not quite mountains but large, expansive, remote and sparsely populated. It is exposed and bleak, but it does have lots of rabbit, grouse, deer and pheasant and is also home to the incredibly shy Northumberland wild goat, so food should not be too hard to come by.

Or do I stay and ride out the storm? With the food in my bugout bag and the emergency supplies I have stacked on shelves in the garage (thank you paranoia-inducing cannabis) I could probably comfortably survive there for around two months, more than enough time for the people in power to sort the situation out.

> I decided I would stay. I had shelter, water and supplies.

> It was a decision I came to regret.

Chapter 5 – The reality check

After checking the TV and internet and finding no change, I chose to check through my local maps to plan out a few escape routes. I promptly dropped off to sleep.

> The next thing I knew I awoke to the sound of gunfire. Fucking gunfire? Here? In England?

> Now that is one of the perks of living in the UK. No guns. The police don't even carry them.

> Unlike in the US, when one goes for the weekly shopping in Blighty, one doesn't have to worry about getting one's fucking face blown off for taking a person's parking space. An altercation in this country is usually sorted out with fisticuffs or at the worst a glass bottle. So, the sound of a gun in the relatively small town of Cramlington was akin to seeing a mackem graduate from university. (Google it.)

Startled, I leapt from my chair and bounded upstairs to my bedroom which overlooked the cul-de-sac (posh for street with a dead end) which I lived on.

In the distance, above the houses on the far side of the housing estate, was some sort of military helicopter hovering around 150 feet from the ground. A soldier was hanging out of the side, tightly gripping a very large mounted gun, pointing and firing it in the general direction of the airport. At this stage I'd like to be able to tell you the type of gun and the size of the projectiles it was spitting out but I didn't have a fucking clue. It was big. And loud.

Some of the neighbours were out in the street staring aghast at the proceedings. I'd love to say I get on well with all of my neighbours. I really would. I hadn't been living among them for very long but they rarely spoke to me or even acknowledged me. Maybe it was because I didn't own a lawn mower, hence the unkempt lawn, and maybe it was because I didn't pull the weeds from the drive, hence making their street (with a dead end) far from perfect. I did return from work one day to find the lawn had been cut for me. Result! They didn't pull up the fucking weeds though. I was sure they'd do it before I did. Maybe not now however.

Anyway, back to the obviously confused neighbours. Waking up to no TV, phone signal, internet or broadcasts of any kind must have been somewhat bewildering. Not to mention the huge fucking whirlybird shooting the shit out of something not too far away.

I opened my window when my closest neighbour Max saw me. He was a nice bloke and one of the only neighbours in the street who didn't look down their nose at me. Always said hello and always had time for a chat. He was probably in his early fifties and took fantastic care of himself fitness wise. He looked at my van parked across the front of the house and waved. 'Whats going on?' he shouted over the roar of the helicopter and gun.

I wished he'd never seen me. I mean, where do you start when explaining the zombie apocalypse to someone who has just woken up? I decided to keep it vague.

'There have been riots all over the country through the night. They think it may be terror related,' I lied. 'Stay inside and lock your doors.'

He looked at me with a mixture of disbelief and humour. Someone else who thinks I'm a bloody joker!

He moved on down the street relaying the information to the other neighbours. Big mistake. As I was watching him do so, and more than likely telling them I was a fruitcake, something caught my eye at the entrance of the street. It was a man.

Now if it had been around midnight on a Saturday the scene before me would not have seemed out of place. Oh, it's just a drunk bloke who looks to have had some sort of argument with the pavement. But no. It was 8am on a Tuesday morning. The man was painfully thin and looked to be in his late eighties and had blood smeared down the bottom half of his face and chest. The neighbours all turned towards him as the man let out a despairing moan. I stood there frozen in my bedroom. Unbelieving. After a whole night of preparing for this moment I was dumbstruck. Unluckily for the neighbours, they weren't. They ran collectively to the aid of the poor, drunken, very old injured man. Before I could come to my senses and warn them, it was too late.

The man lunged towards Max as he approached and grabbed him in bear hug. Now Max is no slouch, gym three times a week and looked to be solid in the muscle department, but no matter how much he tried he couldn't escape the clutches of the rabid pensioner. As Max tried again to pull away, the man went in for his throat with his teeth and tore in to him. The blood and panic that followed were terrifying. I shut my curtains and proceeded to watch through a tiny slit, which offered me, I felt, a degree of safety.

I know what you're thinking. I should have leapt down the stairs and heroically come to the aid of my fellow neighbours and shot crossbow bolts into the old geezer's noggin. Fuck that. I was petrified. Well and truly glued to the spot. I was that scared a little bit of wee came out.

Two of the other neighbours were not so cowardly. They rallied and with great effort broke the death grip between Max and the pensioner and then proceeded to pin the old man down, trying unsuccessfully to avoid his gnashing teeth. The only thing I could think during the carnage was how his teeth were still in his mouth. He was old. Really old. There's no way he didn't have false teeth. Double lashings of Fixadent must have been applied prezombification. Strange, the thoughts that go through your head in perilous situations. Or that might just be me.

While the neighbours were trying to subdue the old man, Max slowly started to get up. 'Oh, thank god,' I thought. 'It must have just been a scratch.'

My jubilation was short lived when Max threw himself upon the struggling neighbours who were holding down the old man. What came next was a blood bath.

By this time the whole street was out, nervously approaching the squirming piles of bodies, not knowing what to do.

I finally pulled myself together and opened the window and shouted over the noise of the still firing helicopter. 'Stay back! Go indoors and lock yourselves in.' At this the neighbours ran back to their respective homes.

I looked back towards the three neighbours and old man to see what was happening and froze. They were all on their feet and staring up at me from across the street! More wee.

Fuck, fuck, fuck. They slowly started shambling their drunken gait towards my house. I shut the curtains again. The first thing I heard was the slapping of hands on my van outside and then that god-awful moaning. I'm not going to lie. I started crying. All my false bravado and silly excitement gone. This was real. I didn't want to be bitten. I'd been bitten before in a play fight with the ex and it hurt like buggery. And she didn't even break the skin. Also, please let it be known that I have no idea what buggery feels like but I can imagine it hurts as much as a play-fight bite.

I crept downstairs and carefully sneaked a peak through the bay window curtains. Most of my view was obscured by the van but I could see the old man banging away on the bonnet with his fists. I knew there was no way they could get into the house from the front so I did what any other person would do who'd had my vast survival training and expertise. I went and hid in the cupboard under the stairs. Yep, that's right.

All those years of role-playing scenarios about what I would do if the zombies came, I never once hid under the stairs with pissy pants.

Chapter 6   The alterations

After a while I summoned up enough courage, came out from the cupboard and sneaked another peek between the gap in the curtains. I found that the helicopter had stopped shooting and fled and, to my surprise, the monsters had left too. WTF?

I ran upstairs and looked out of the bedroom window to confirm that they had really gone. They were still in the street but had moved to another house and were frantically banging on the doors and windows. I knew the neighbour who lived there. She was called Alice I think. A rotund middle-aged lady who'd actually shaken her head at me one day while admiring the weeds on my drive. It was mainly her fault that I hadn't got around to tidying the garden. I can be a little stubborn at times and have been known to cut my nose off to spite my face.

The silly cow must have drawn the monsters away from my house somehow.

From what I could see of the zombies. No, let's stop a minute and think of a better name. Zombie has been done to death. (Pardon the pun.) Walkers? No that's been used before. Creepers? So has that. All the good names have been used so I shall have to invent one but now is not the time. On with the story.

The zombies, on closer inspection looked, acted and moved like all the zombies I'd ever read about. Slow, ungainly, covered in blood with parts of their anatomy bitten away and all of them emitting that unearthly moan. Apart from Max of course, he had no fucking larynx left.

And before you start, I know there have been other books and films which contain fast, running and jumping zombies. I refused to ever read or watch them on principle. I like my zombies old school. Romero style!

The zombies I was now viewing, as they battered away at Alice's front door, were proper old school. Slow and thick as shit. Just the way I like 'em. So what should I call them? Well, seeing as I'm a Geordie I've decided on deedaz (that translates into 'deaders' if you're from daan saaf).

I began to realise slowly that the deedaz in my street weren't an imminent threat to me at that moment and would have to start putting one of my plans into action before any more of the clumsy shambling fucks showed up.

The house was as secure as it was ever going to be. There was no way they could get in from the front, but if enough of them pushed up against my flimsy garage door, it would buckle and may allow them access to the garden through the door at the back of the garage, which had always been the weak point in my plan of staying put. As quickly as possible I moved all of my supplies upstairs, piled them into the spare room and went back into the garage to retrieve some tools, my extendable ladders and some 2 x 4 wood I'd been meaning to throw out.

My idea was to shore up the back door with the 2 x 4 and then quietly dismantle the stairs up to the first floor of the house. I say quietly. There was nothing quiet about me hammering the 2 x 4 into the door frame and absolutely nothing quiet when it came to demolishing the stairs. I decided to take the first ten steps out and did so with a crow bar after I'd removed the carpet. I was surprised at how easily they came up. Having done that, I stripped away the plaster board from the ceiling inside of the cupboard under the stairs, took the door off and then stood back and admired my handy work. The landlord would go fuckin' ballistic if he could see what I'd done. He'd have to take this off my bond too.

Once the dust had settled and the noise abated, I realised the slapping of hands on the van had started again.

I set the ladders up against the first stair I'd left in place, around two and a half metres from the ground, and climbed up to go and take a look out of my bedroom window to see if Max and his buddies had returned. What I saw chilled me to the bone. The whole street had deedaz milling around outside different neighbours' houses. Some of Alice's windows were broken and the deedaz were trying to drag themselves through. Alice was futilely pushing back against the tide with a sturdy garden broom. I looked down towards my van and saw what can only be described as the pit of hell. More wee I'm afraid. I promised myself at that moment, if I ever made it out of there I'd go straight to a pharmacy and purchase some fucking tenaladies. (google it.)

Chapter 7   The bloodbath

Before me stood around thirty of them. Mostly dressed in nightgowns and slippers, they started pushing and shoving the van. It was rocking so much on its suspension that it started banging off the wall of the house. Which in turn made noise, which in turn attracted more deedaz towards my humble domicile. The entrance to the street was now full of them. Where the fuck did they all come from? Then I remembered how fast Max had turned into one of them. It felt like seconds but was probably a couple of minutes.

Now usually, in all the best zombie novels, you got bitten then over a couple of days you got the flu, died and then came back as the walking dead. That usually gave the person a little time to come to terms with his or her inevitable doom. But not the deedaz. You got bitten, you turned straight away. No more, 'I'm bitten, you go on and I'll hold them back' from your fellow survivors. This was a case of, as soon as someone gets bitten you quickly and decisively cave their fucking skulls in. No time for sentiment or goodbyes. Just a good old-fashioned caving.

My decision to stay at the house was fast becoming the wrong one. The first rule of zombie is mobility. Being mobile is always one of the best ways of staying alive when it comes to the Z.A. No one ever survives in a static location. In all the films and books I've watched or read, the tenacity of the dead always overcomes. They never give up and never get tired. I should have known better, what with my vast knowledge of everything zombie related.

Nothing I could do about that now. By the look of things, half the town was infected and converging on my house.

A blood-curdling scream echoed down the street from Alice's house. The deedaz had grabbed her brush and instead of letting her trusty weapon go, she hung on for some reason and was dragged kicking and screaming out of the broken window. I turned away from the ensuing free-for-all and clapped my hands over my ears to blot out the heart-wrenching screams of agony that came from Alice. It was over in seconds. I opened one eye then the other, scanning the crowd in Alice's front garden for any signs of her. Nothing. She was gone. Literally ripped to shreds by the ghouls.

Others neighbours in the street must have witnessed this and in panic tried to run from their houses and get into their vehicles. The collective moan from the deedaz was tremendous as they converged on to the panicking residents. They never stood a chance and soon fell the way of Alice. One man actually made it in to his car and floored it towards a large crowd of deedaz who had entered the street, probably attracted by Alice's last scream.

    The impact was immense. Bodies flew everywhere but there were just too many to plough through and he came to an abrupt stop. He had obviously not strapped his seat belt on and came crashing through the windscreen. Initially unconscious, he awoke to the sight of a hundred hands pulling out his lower intestine. There just wasn't enough room for them all to get a bite, so hands reached in from the throng that surrounded him and ripped and tore at his flesh. I'm sure he would have screamed if part of his diaphragm hadn't been scooped out and quickly devoured by one of the deedaz. The agony on his face disappeared and then, as if a switch had been flipped, the deedaz that were feasting on him suddenly stopped and moved away. WTF? Had he died then turned or turned before he died?

    The man slowly rolled from the bonnet of the car and started crawling towards the sounds of breaking glass and moans further down the street. After losing all of his abdominal muscles his only form of locomotion was to crawl. I'd have to think of a name for the crawly ones.

Things were getting out of hand. None of the drama that had been going on in the street had seemed to deter the deedaz on my lawn. They were still hammering away at my poor van, which was now absolutely covered in bloody handprints.

Crack! Crunch! Bang!

It sounded like my fucking garage door had just given up the ghost. I looked to my right where the garage was located and could see a throng of deedaz entering it. Shit. Hopefully the door into the garden from the garage would hold them back. They were one step closer to breaching my meagre defences. Plan B would have to be implemented!

Chapter 8   The move

After pulling the ladders up I erected them under the loft hatch. I'd never actually been up there before so didn't know what to expect. I slid the hatch to one side and climbed up. Something brushed past my face. I screamed and pulled away, then laughed a little when I realised what it was and pulled it. The lights came on.

To my surprise the loft space was boarded and was fairly large. Enough room to stand up straight in the centre. I quickly began ferrying all of my supplies up the ladder. I added a bucket too for poos. Better safe than sorry. If they did somehow enter the house and navigate up the dismantled staircase I now had another fall-back position and a place to take a dump. I knew that if they did enter the house I was proper, proper fucked.

Once I was up there I had virtually no access to the van or the gallons of water in the bath tub. The bottled water I had would only last a month and a half or so. I'd think of something. I hoped.

Once the supplies were moved I took a look out of the rear upstairs window to see if they'd broken into the garden. The good news was they hadn't. The bad news was the banging from the van against the house reverberated right down to the foundations and was attracting more and more of them. Again, the more noise the van made, the harder they pushed, the greater the noise.

It was now around lunchtime and the stress of all that had happened was starting to catch up, plus the fact that I'd moved all the supplies up two flights of stairs. Pun alert! I was dead on my feet.

I decided to change my pissy pants, have a bite to eat using the perishables I had in the fridge, sit on the bed and think about my next course of action.

How I dropped off to sleep with the racket they were making I'll never know. Adrenaline is a good thing to have but once it wears off, exhaustion will hit you like a ton of bricks.

Chapter 9 – The unpleasant surprise

I awoke with a start, wondering if it had all been a dream. Unfortunately, the sound of the incessant moaning outside shattered that wonder. The banging had ceased, which was good news I suppose. I looked at my watch and realised I'd slept for around three hours. I checked the view outside the front window. No change. They were still there but were aimlessly bumping into each other and going nowhere. I checked the back window. No change there, the garden was still clear. Checked my phone signal.

No change. Checked the internet connection. No change. Nothing.

I pondered at why everything had come to an abrupt halt with regard to the media shutdown. It was probably a government thing. To keep us from panicking while they got things under control. Instead of just being honest and informing everyone of what precautions to take, they kept everyone in the dark and condemned the lot of us.

I decided to rectify the water problem I would have if they actually did breach the stairs and find their way up to the first floor. I replaced the ladders, lowering them carefully and quietly to the ground floor, and crept into the kitchen in search of pans and vessels to fill with water from the bathroom. The pots and pans cupboard was situated under the kitchen window next to the sink. I crouched down and opened it and silently withdrew the largest ones. With that done I closed the cupboard door and stood up.

To my utter disbelief, my eyes fell upon a hideously disfigured deeda standing opposite me on the other side of the window in the back garden. At first I think it was just as surprised as me. I say 'it' because there were no discernible features that could determine its sex. Its face and scalp had been torn off, leaving only bare muscle and sinew behind. It stood there staring with its white film-covered eyes but soon came out of its surprised stupor when I dropped the pans and pots from fright at the sight of the thing.

A hideous howl came from what was left of its mouth, to be joined by a chorus of moans from its brethren. They'd breached the fucking garden!

I slunk down on the floor against the cupboard and hid again. Thankfully I didn't piss myself this time. I don't think I had anything left in my bladder after the morning I'd had.

Seconds later a cacophony of slapping hands against the window startled me into action. I quickly scooped up the pans, ran for the ladders and scooted back to the first floor and pulled the ladders up behind me. A quick glance through the spare bedroom window explained how they'd broken into the back garden. The door to the garage was wide open.

I'd shut it the last time I was in there but didn't lock it. Stupid.

They were either smarter than the average zombie or had somehow accidentally opened it. Shit.

There was a crash from downstairs. It sounded like a window. FUCK! Had I locked the back door to the house? What if they repeated the garage door trick? The 2 x 4s I'd nailed would hold for a little while but would last a lot longer if the door was locked. Should I go back and check? I decided if it bought me some extra time and stemmed the flow of deedaz coming into the house it was worth the risk.

I know you're now in the process of saying, 'NFW, stay where you are you daft Geordie bastard,' but I had to. I looped the machete sheath through my belt and tightened it. Then did a couple of practice draws in the mirror to check the best position of it and also to see if I looked tough, which on reflection meant nothing to the dead. All they saw was walking raw meat and would not be intimidated by my furrowed brow and curled lip. But for some reason it did give me the confidence I needed to go back downstairs.

I lowered the ladders and slowly edged my way down, looking through the rungs towards the kitchen. The noise emanating from the back garden was thunderous and there was also an awful smell seeping through the door that separated the living room and kitchen. At first I thought I might have soiled myself, it was that bad. I wouldn't have been surprised to be honest. My bodily functions seemed to have a mind of their own at the time.

I would liken the smell that was obviously emanating from the deedaz, to shit mixed with sour milk and rotten eggs.

I dry heaved as I gingerly walk towards the kitchen and was welcomed by an audience of around thirty faces pushed up against the back door and the kitchen window, which had been partially smashed. When they saw me, they became frantic and looked at me with angry, evil, milky eyes. The door shook on its hinges. If they could remember how to open doors they'd have tried the handle by now so it was only a matter of time before a stray arm did the honours for them. I ran for the door and quickly turned the key to the left to lock it.

It was already locked. Bollocks!

I'd found out years ago that another side effect of long-term cannabis use was short-term memory loss. Entering rooms and forgetting what I went in for was a common occurrence with my hash ravaged mind and would annoyingly happen on average around three times a day.

I about-faced and ran for the ladders just as the back door and the 2 x 4s succumbed to the pressure of the deedaz with an ear-splitting crash. It probably would have held if I hadn't advertised myself like an all you can eat buffet by going back.

When I was small my dad, rest his soul, used to pretend to be a monster and chase me round the house for fun. On the odd occasion I would choose the stairs as my avenue of escape. I don't know if you've ever been chased upstairs before, but for some reason it is absolutely fucking terrifying. There's nothing to hide behind, nowhere else to go but up and nothing to throw at your pursuers. My dad would always let me reach the last step before he would grab my foot, trip me up and proceed to tickle me till I wet myself. Yes, I've always had a weak bladder.

Well now I was having a flashback of epic proportions. Only this time it wasn't my dad chasing me, and the outcome of getting caught wasn't a jolly good tickling ending up with wet pants, it was death by a thousand teeth and ending up with wet, shitty and bloody pants.

I ran as fast as my jelly legs would carry me and scrambled up the ladders. True to form, as I reached the top rung, a hand grabbed my ankle. I turned, lay on my back and kicked at its wrist with my other foot. Luckily, I must have broken something in its arm because it suddenly let go and fell. I quickly pulled up the steps inches from the grasp of a dozen hands then pushed away from the stairs and took a deep breath, gagged on the stench and counted my lucky stars that I hadn't been dragged into the maelstrom of deedaz down below.

Chapter 10 – The uninvited

The living room was full to the brim of the stinking bastards. The malodorous stench that blasted up with venom was akin to pepper spray. I know this because I have been the victim of the supposedly humane crowd control device.

    It was at an away game. The first and last I ever went to. I actually never even made it to the game. My friend and I caught the train and had unintentionally booked onto the same carriage as the local football hooligans. They were called the gremlins. And a bunch of tough looking fuckers they were too. Luckily for us we had our colours on. They seemed like a happy bunch at the beginning but the closer we got to our destination the more the atmosphere started to change. The conductor had stopped coming into the carriage, along with the trolley dolly, who'd run out of alcoholic beverages around the same time we passed Darlington, which was probably only twenty minutes from the station we'd left from. This didn't go down well with the gremlins who took umbrage at this by throwing empty beer cans at the conductor.

    Eventually the train started to slow for our station. As we pulled in, the police presence on the platform was astounding. The conductor must have called ahead so the police were ready for our arrival. As soon as the doors opened they stormed in. The gremlins, realising that their chance of a ruck with the home supporters was at an end, decided it would be fun instead to rumble with the plod. And that was when I was pepper sprayed. Apparently being in the same carriage as the hooligans was reason enough for the filth to mace the whole fucking lot of us.

It was by far one of the worst experiences of my life. No breath could be had, my eyes stung like mad and my nose ran buckets. This feeling lasted for over an hour and I received absolutely no sympathy from the miserable fucking desk sergeant at the local nick. Eventually we were released without charge or an apology. We were told we should have moved carriages before the police boarded the train. I told them I would have done if I'd known the Iranian embassy siege was about to be re-enacted in front me. He didn't find it funny. I did.

And here I was. In my own home, eyes watering, gasping for breath with snot everywhere while evil flesh-eating dead people wrecked my living room. I don't think the bond will cover this one. Sorry Mr landlord.

The decision to go straight for the loft came easily. There was no way I could stand the stink. I filled the pans with water and carefully took them up. I also emptied my wardrobe and took as many items of clothing up there as I could. Pillows and duvet followed. Eventually safe in the loft with all my supplies I pulled up the step ladders and replaced the wooden board over the hole. I'd soaked some towels in the bath before ascending and rolled them up to cover the frame of the hatch. Hopefully to stop the stomach-churning stench filtering through and maybe limit the noise of the dead fucks. Maybe without prey in their midst they may forget about me after a while and fuck right off.

Chapter 11 – The siege

It was two days before the outer ranks that were at the entrance to the garage started to filter away. I know this because I stripped a corner of insulation from inside of the roof above me and forced some of the roof tiles out of the way. Just enough to get my head and shoulders through. I could smell that the throng in the living room was still there in full force but they had quietened down a lot since they lost sight of me. The deedaz that wandered off were attracted to a faint humming noise I could hear in the distance. It sounded like an engine in full revs but it wasn't loud enough to draw the rest away.

The previous two days had given me a lot of time to watch and study the revenants that wandered the street. Most of them had very few injuries. The odd bite here and there. Mostly on the forearms. The ones that had been really disfigured must have been set upon by a multitude of attackers. The deedaz seemed to lose interest in eating the victim as soon as it turned which, by my estimation judging by Max's transformation, was under thirty seconds after he'd first been bitten. There was nothing left of Alice to turn.

I also deduced that the deedaz became excited if they were stimulated either by sight or sound. At the time I didn't think their other senses worked anymore and that they surely couldn't smell their prey because of the awful stench coming from their own putrid decomposing bodies. I didn't think they could taste either. I saw one of them tucking in to Alice's lower colon and that was full of shit, so taste was definitely out. Nor do I think they could feel pain or do they fear for their own self-preservation. They didn't bat an eye when that car tried to make a break for it and ploughed into them at the end of the street. They just got up, if they could, and attacked. The ones with legs beyond repair simply dragged themselves around the ground looking for scraps. There were no cries of agony from any of the deedaz.

Apart from the odd curtain twitch I had neither seen nor heard another surviving neighbour. I had heard uncountable screams from other residents of Cramlington and a lot of car horns, but two days later I was left only with the distant moaning of the damned and the engine noise in the distance.

The supply situation was going considerably well. Mainly because I wasn't eating that much. The towels I had used to block the gaps around the loft hatch had dried out and the ammonia laced aroma of the deedaz in my living room was seeping through and ruining my appetite. I could go down to the first floor and soak them again in the bath tub but risked arousing the dead fucks from their partial stasis.

Hours turned into days turned into weeks turned into a month and there I was still living like a hermit. Shitting in a bucket and pouring the contents out of the hole I'd made in the roof. If this thing ever blows over and things go back to normal, I must make a note not to clean those gutters. Eeww.

The boredom was the worst thing. Endless hours of being afraid and thinking about the different ways you may reach your eventual demise can drive a person mad.

The daylight hours were passed by reading under the natural light that entered through the hole in the roof. I still had lots of candles left but refused to light more than one per night and reading was virtually impossible with a single tea light.

Luckily I'd had the foresight to take with me my collection of every *Trail* magazine printed in the last ten years. Although being able to ever visit the places and mountains featured in the publications was highly unlikely to ever happen.

Believe it or not the only thing I truly missed was the gym. Of course I missed a normal life and all it entails, i.e. not fearing for your safety every second of the day. But I'd never been much of a people person. Yes, I had a lot friends but wasn't really close to any of them. I'd keep myself to myself most of the time and the only person who really knew me was the ex. When talking to random people at work or out and about, I used the same old phrases and conversation topics time and again. I always got the feeling when talking with people that they weren't actually listening to what I said, they were just coming up with ways to insert their own agenda into the conversation. Never asking questions, just wanting to big themselves up.

So the solitude I was experiencing while being forced to live in the loft was something that didn't really affect me as much as it should. Well, maybe I missed people a little, but not as much as I missed the gym.

    As you've probably realised by now, I have a serious problem with addiction. My addiction at the time was fitness. Not a bad addiction to have, I know, but as you can probably guess, I took it a little too far. I'd spend an hour in the morning, an hour at lunch time and two hours at night in the gym. Interspersed with lots and lots of running. In the space of a year I'd lost nearly four stone and at forty-two was the fittest I'd ever been in my life. Sigmund would say I wasn't doing it for myself, I was doing it for the ex. Maybe if I was fitter than her new boyfriend, Mr Fucking Motivator, she'd lose interest in him and want me back. Perhaps he's right. All I knew was, when I was exercising, it was the only time I didn't think about her. I think that's what I was probably addicted to at first. Now, however, being able to look in a full-length mirror and not see man boobs was what I craved, so Mr Freud could suck a fart right out of my arse!

    My food supplies were still plentiful but the water situation was becoming a problem. I had been washing myself every day with wet wipes, but the majority of my food had been dehydrated and needed to be soaked in water to make it edible. The water from the pans I'd retrieved had lasted for a week and a half. If I was desperate I could get some from the bath but I didn't really trust the water in there anymore. It had become stagnant and god knows what else was in it. The house wasn't exactly clean at the moment with all my guests downstairs and the risk of airborne particles floating upstairs from them and landing in the exposed bath were too great. The bathwater would definitely have to be a last resort. It would have to be thoroughly boiled before consumption and would have made a rather large dent in my portable gas supply.

    Also, the weather had been uncharacteristically dry all summer. Here in the northeast, summer usually lasted for around a week during the month of May. The rest of the time it pissed down with rain. I'd laid a tarp out on the roof that faced the back garden and folded the bottom corners inward so as to funnel rain water down through a six-inch hole I'd made in the roof. Underneath the hole was one of the large containers. The trouble was the lack of rain. The condensation that accrued on it every morning wasn't even enough for a mouthful. The effort it took to squeegee the minute droplets down to the funnel made it not worth the while.

All utilities had ceased around about the same time after the first week. I know this because at first I thought the bulb in the loft had blown but then noticed the street lights had stopped working too. This wasn't too much of a problem and the candles would suffice as long as I didn't burn the place down.

I knew the water mains were off because the severely leaky tap I'd asked the landlord to fix, on three separate occasions, had finally stopped dripping. Every cloud has a silver lining I suppose.

After I'd read my library of magazines for the third time and with the smell drifting in from the shit in the roof gutter, thoughts of the best way to commit suicide started popping into my head. I decided enough was enough.

> A line from a song by the Geordie super group 'The Animals' popped into my mind.

> 'We gotta get out of this place, if it's the last thing we ever do!'

Chapter 12 – The outing

Planning my exodus from the confines of the loft space was frustrating, simply because I had no intel on the situation outside of my street. For all I knew the roads and cycle path system throughout the estate were packed with wandering dead fucks or clogged up with escaping cars that didn't make it out past the congestion of panicking survivors on the roads. It could be absolute mayhem out there. The last thing I wanted was to speed out of the street in the van, turn the corner and become stranded in traffic. I had no plan for embarking in the van at that time but I was sure I'd come up with something if the roads were clear enough to escape. I needed to do some reconnaissance before I leapt into a decision of this magnitude.

I got to work.

The street I lived in, as I explained before, is a cul-de-sac which consists of semidetached houses with garages on each side which are then connected to the garages of the next pair of semidetached houses. So technically the houses aren't detached at all, it's more of a terrace row with garages that sweep around in an arc shape.

My home was exactly four plots away from the entrance to the street. If I'd lived in the house directly opposite me I would have had an unrestricted view of the main road exiting the estate from its roof. But I didn't. I needed to get to that house to see if an escape with the van would be viable.

The street was still full of deedaz milling around, so going down and through them was out of the question. The only way I could think of doing it was to roof hop. A little like the garden hopping I used to do with my friends when I was young. One of the most exhilarating and favourite pastimes of my youth. That and knocky door ginger.

The aim of garden hopping was to get from one end of a street to the other without getting caught by the owners of the gardens we ran through. The only differences between garden hopping and roof hopping were that I'd be carrying the ladders for the roofs and if I got caught by anyone I wouldn't be frog marched around to my mum by the ear. I'd be torn to shreds!

Luckily all of the garages were flat. The only dangers that faced me were if a stray foot went through a house

roof or falling off and breaking my neck. Which would be preferable to falling off and breaking my leg, which would condemn me to a fate worse than death, i.e.
being eaten alive

It was still summer, the roofs were dry so slipping shouldn't be a problem. The problem was attracting the dead fucks with the noise I would surely make.

I decided I would set off a couple of hours before sunrise. At this time of the year it never really got pitch black dark so hopefully I could be there and back before it got too bright. I set the alarm on my watch and lay down on my not so clean duvet and got some shuteye.

After waking I readied myself and had a bite to eat before I left. I climbed through the hole in the roof, pulled the ladders out, climbed to the apex and shuffled down the side facing the back garden. Most of the other back gardens were empty, although mine had a fair few deedaz aimlessly standing in and around the flower beds. Or should I say weed beds.

I quietly lowered the ladders down to the garage roof. I had wrapped the dried towels, that were on the loft hatch, around the feet and top of the ladders and secured them with lashings of gaffer tape. Hopefully this would deaden the sound when set up against the walls.

Taking the utmost care and without making any noise it took me ten minutes to climb down, walk quietly along the garages and climb up to next door neighbour's roof.

There were twelve of these gaps I had to navigate to reach the opposite house. At this rate it was going to take much longer than two hours to get there, scope the road and get back. It wasn't too late to go back and try a little earlier the next night, but the shit was starting to pile high in my gutter and I wanted to get out of that loft ASAP.

It took me well over an hour and a half to reach the house. I got in to a rhythm after the first couple of houses and did so without making a squeak. It was all for nought though. I climbed the last roof and stood open mouthed at the carnage before me.

There were cars everywhere. Roads and paths were full of them. Total gridlock. Doors askew. Blood covered everything, with the deedaz wandering through the mess checking interiors for meat.

I sat down and sobbed. The loss of life had been immense judging from the rivers of congealed blood. As I turned from the grotesque sight and prepared for the long climb back, I glanced down into the bicycle track that wound its way throughout the estate and saw it was clear of cars. Also, the entrance to the track was blocked by a large removal van. There were a few deedaz waddling down the enclosed path but not as many as in the streets and in my house. I decided if I was going to leave this would have to be my escape route and hoped the cycle path's other narrow entrances around the estate were similarly inaccessible.

On my way back to my house I saw that the house two down from me backed onto a field that one of the cycling tracks ran through. This part of the track was somehow free of zombies as far as I could tell. Deciding my best course of action would be to collect my bugout bag and vacate through this avenue of least resistance, I climbed the remaining houses and made it back to my humble if not stinking abode.

.

Chapter 13   The experiment

I'd been clocked by the deedaz down in the street and they had somehow zeroed in on my house and began to filter through the garage and into the garden again. Once back inside and as quietly as I could I opened the loft hatch and peeked down. Seconds after I did the dead fucks downstairs let out a collective moan that shook my bones. Somehow they'd heard me. I was so quiet though. Had something in them changed?

Before I decided to leave, an experiment would be needed to resolve my suspicions. If they were changing I needed to know before I took flight.

How had they detected me? It couldn't have been with those milky excuses they called eyes. Unless the milky film was some sort of science fucktion infrared shit! I hoped not.

I lowered the ladders down through the loft hatch, taking no care in how much noise I made. They knew I was there so I wasn't going to waste energy gently lowering myself down. I entered my bedroom and retrieved a large jar from under the bed. In it was an accumulation of around one year's worth of coins from nightly emptied pockets. Before I climbed back into the loft I spared a peek down the broken stairs. My heart stopped. There in front of me, from the waist up, was a deeda. Had they learned to fucking fly now? When my heart finally started beating I realised it was standing on the bodies of other deedaz. The tide of dead I'd created when hopping the houses had crushed the deedaz together so tightly they'd made a bridge of death. Zombies from the kitchen had somehow climbed up and for want of a better phrase were fucking crowd surfing toward the broken stairs.

The zombie, at seeing live flesh, scrambled up towards me. I turned and ran for the steps. Again, that awful sensation of being chased by my dad panicked me in to virtually jumping up in to the loft. All this with the jar of coins in tow. Why I didn't drop them, I'll never know. Just as I made it through the hatch I heard the clatter of the ladders falling.

Fuck!

I mean, I could probably manage without the ladders. The drop from the roof to the garage wasn't far but I'd planned on roof hopping to the house that backed onto the field and cycle path. I could always drop into next door's garden from their garage and climb over the fences between to get to the cycle track, but what if my route was blocked by my adoring fans? I'd never be able to get back to the relative safety of my loft. There was nothing for it. Adapt and overcome.

Decisions had to be made. Firstly, I had to ascertain what abilities the deedaz had 'evolved', if any. I took the coins to the hole in the roof took out a pund chunk (pound coin) and lobbed it as far as I could. It landed with a clatter on top of the car that had crashed on the day this all started. Every head that was still in the street turned towards the car followed by an unearthly chorus of wailing from the putrid bastards. A stumbling tsunami of flesh converged on the car looking for the source of the noise the coin had made. As soon as they arrived at the car and realised nothing warm was around they fell silent. Well at least they hadn't suddenly found the skill of sprinting. Still old school. Thank fuck.

The next coin made it past the car and hit the curb opposite, making a much lesser noise. Like meerkats the dead turned en masse at the sound and moved again. Next, I threw a coin on to the grass. The dull thud it made was virtually undetectable. If they homed in on that then I was fucked. Proper proper proper fucked.

Luckily none of them turned. So, super zombie radar hearing was not the reason they had gone ape shit when I slid the loft hatch open. Sight wasn't the reason either. The view of the loft hatch from the living room was slightly obscured by the wall. That realistically only left scent. Could they smell me from all the way downstairs through the loft hatch? And so quickly? And with the smell of rotten milkyeggpoo rising from them? The only conclusion I came up with was the draft from the hole in the roof must have drawn my scent through the hatch and taken it through the house and out of the back door. This resulted in an evergrowing ruckus and attracted more of them from the street and into the garage.

Now as you know, I'd been stuck in that loft for over a month and had regularly cleaned myself with wet wipes, but to say I was ripe would be an understatement. The clean clothes I'd taken with me into the loft had all been worn twice over. I had spare clothes in the bugout bag but they were for emergency use only. The only thing I had left that didn't stink of body odour and bum was a camouflaged onesie that the ex had bought me to go with the survival course she'd given me for my fortieth birthday. That would have to do. I'd look like a fucking lunatic but I didn't think the zombies would mind. They'd probably still smell me if they were close but with a bit of luck, the right wind direction and a jolly good wiping down I might just escape unscathed.

Chapter 14   The inevitable journey

The dilemma now was where to go when I reached the cycle path. As the crow flies the town I live in is around five miles west of the coast. Once there I could maybe find a boat and sail/motor to any one of the numerous islands along the coastline or maybe get picked up by some fellow survivors. I'm no seaman but understood the principles of sailing. How hard could it be to follow the beach while out at sea? Lots of things to eat there too, and fresh water if I timed the tides correctly and sailed far enough up any of the multitude of rivers along the way. And as far as I knew the deedaz couldn't swim. I hoped.

    The other option, as I explained earlier, was to head for the hills. Yes, there were some pros to going that way but it would be over a thirty-mile walk through a land of the living dead. And no guarantee, when I got there, of finding a stronghold to keep me safe.

Most people would hoof it to the nearest shopping centre where there's lots of food and equipment to be had. Which brings us to one of the first rules of zombie invasion. Never travel through or to populated areas. Which was something I was about to do. Cramlington is one of the largest towns in the county of Northumberland. Fortunately, my estate was on the outskirts and with luck I could be in a farmer's field and on my way to wherever I needed within ten minutes.

I deliberated for most of the day and came to a decision as it started to get dark.

A sailor's life for me!

I rose early and took the next few hours to prepare my kit, and by noon I was ready for the journey. I'd decided to risk travelling by day instead of night. I'll admit the darkness would make me less likely to be seen but that works both ways. I'd rather be able to see what was eating me than get chewed on in the dark

Onesie on, tactical belt with both machete and hatchet looped on, bugout bag on. And I was ready.

I managed to squeeze through the hole in the roof, lowered myself over the edge of the gable end, let go and fell around five feet to the garage roof. There was no point trying to keep quiet at this stage. This escape was to be a shock and awe mission. To just run like fuckery before they knew what was happening. I crossed over onto next door's adjoining garage roof, quickly checked their garden was clear and dropped into it. The boundary between our houses was part brick and part fence, the upper part being fence. No sooner had I dropped, than the deedaz in my garden started assaulting it. It gave in seconds, but since the wall was just above waist height, the sudden surge of the dead made sure the ones in the front line of the assault were pinned by the ones behind, unable to climb or fall over. This gave me enough time to scale the opposite fence and partake in my favourite schoolboy pastime.

As soon as I was out of sight of the dead they stopped their frantic wails. I popped my head over to see what was happening. When they saw me they started up again. I quickly ducked. No sooner had I done so than they calmed. The wind direction was slight but it was travelling from the deedaz towards me. They obviously couldn't smell me. Without constant stimulation and without means to pursue it seemed the saying 'out of sight out of mind' was true. They'd follow prey in its general direction even if they lost sight of it, but if an obstruction got in their way during the chase they seemed to go into hibernation mode and forget about the target.

Working my way over the next two fences I entered the garden that backed on to the cycle track. As I prepared to exit I turned towards the house, readied myself and took a deep breath before opening the gate. The curtain in an upstairs window moved. I waited and watched. It moved again. There was someone up there. Someone alive.

Chapter 15   The thin lady

The fact that there was someone alive in my street astounded me. I hadn't seen hide nor hair of anyone since two days after the initial event. I heard the screams of the attacked and dying and had noticed most of the doors and windows in the street had been broken and smashed. So the fact someone had survived this long was a surprise to say the least.

I waited to see if they showed themselves. I didn't know who lived here, so when a sad emaciated face appeared at the window there was no recognition from me at all. And even if I did know her I don't know if I'd have been able to recognise her anyway. She was obviously on the verge of starvation. Skeletal was too kind a description of her. She mouthed the word 'help' through the gap in the curtains. I motioned for her to open the window and I went and stood underneath it. With great difficulty she opened it about an inch. 'Do you need help?' I whispered. She nodded. 'Can you come down and let me in?' She shook her head frantically this time.

'I want to help, I won't hurt you'. Shaking her head, she weakly pointed over her shoulder to where her bedroom door obviously was.

'Are they in the house?' I whispered. She mouthed back 'My husband'. Now either he was very possessive and didn't like his wife talking to men or he was deader than a fucking dodo and was in the house with her. She had obviously barricaded herself in the bedroom when her husband had turned. When this happened was anyone's guess but if I had to, it was probably around two to three weeks ago judging by how gaunt she was. She must have had access to water because the average person can last around three weeks without food and she looked close to that mark.

'I'm leaving. Do you want to come with me?' She looked at me as if I was mad. It was probably a stupid question but I had to ask it. For one, I think if I'd said boo to her she'd have dropped down dead and two, I don't think she'd make it to the end of the garden under her own steam. 'Do you need some food?' She nodded vigorously.

There was no way she was having what I had in my bugout bag. I'd have to somehow retrace my route and go back to the loft. There was still a good few weeks' worth of supplies left. She could have them. All I had to do was find a ladder.

'I'm going to go and get you some food and water, I'll be back soon.' Wrong thing to say. She panicked and started banging on the window as I turned away. 'Don't leave me,' she rasped.

Suddenly a banging came from within the house. 'Oh no!' was all she said as I looked up into her terrified eyes.

A crash followed, she screamed and then she was gone, undoubtedly in an eternal embrace from her husband.

I stood there shocked. Again I had done nothing but watch. I'd never have reached her in time in any case, but this was starting to become a habit. My indecision and inability to act under pressure were becoming more apparent to me and were fast becoming a worrying trait. All the years of mental zombie practice had been a waste of time. Under pressure I was lacking everything I needed to stay alive. Split-second decision making was obviously not one of my strong points. The only thing I'd been able to do since this event started was to hide, run and piss myself. Doubt in my abilities was beginning to grow exponentially. Should I just find a ladder and return to my little cave in the loft? I had a few weeks of food left and could probably scrounge some water from some of the other houses on the street. Maybe the government would get this under control? Maybe they're just working their way up the country exterminating this threat to humanity. Maybe in a few days' time everything would be back to normal. Maybe the ex would forgive me and tell Sporticus to fuck right off. Nope. None of that was going to happen.

I either continued with my plan or I stayed and died of thirst or starvation in the stinking roof space of my house.

I built up enough courage to tiptoe back to the gate leading to the cycle path, looked over the top and saw nothing in the vicinity. It was now or never. I unlocked and opened the gate, taking a quick glance up to the window where I'd first seen Skeletor. Looking down at me were the unhappy couple. They just stood there watching me with accusing eyes. He was looking a little worse for wear and she looked like Stephen fucking King's 'Carrie'. Totally creeped out and with a heavy and guilt-ridden heart I turned and stepped beyond the gate.

Chapter 16   The gauntlet

The quickest way to the coast was east, but that would take me through the majority of the vast housing estate I lived on. I headed north along the cycle path which was the fastest way to open ground and the fields beyond. I'd have to cross a dual carriageway but would worry about that if I ever got out of the estate. Usually it would take around five minutes to get there at a jog, but things had changed a lot since then. With machete in my right hand and my crossbow in the other, in case I needed to do some stealthy shit, I hugged the fence alongside the path. Slowly and quietly I made my way north.

After a few minutes, I spotted in the distance and to the left of my route a small group of deedaz gathered around something on the ground. I checked the wind direction and gauged that it was blowing slightly towards me. They wouldn't smell me but I was out in the open and if they looked up for a second they would definitely see me. The dual carriage way was around a three-minute run away from my present location. Two minutes if I legged it. The only problem I might have was at the end of the path. It bottle necked into a narrow cut between two houses. If that was blocked or if there were deedaz there I'd be trapped. At the end of the path was a lightly wooded area on a slight incline. Once I got through that, the main road would be accessible. I decided that discretion would not be the best part of valour. My pack was full and heavy but was strapped tight to my body. I clipped the crossbow back on it and withdrew my hatchet. If it came to it I'd hack my way through.

Deep breath, weapons in hand and a quick prayer (I am an atheist by the way but I'm also a gambling man and like to hedge my bets) and I was off. As soon as I started running, heads turned towards me. Yes, you guessed it, a little bit of wee came out. I ran along the right side of the path opposite the little mothers meeting they were having. Slowly they started to rise, and with it came the god-awful moaning. To my left and right the call was answered in some of the gardens I ran past. I'd inadvertently rung the bell for dinner time. I ran past the group, which consisted of around five or six, and got a glimpse of what had held their rapturous attention. I think it was human. There was ribcage here, a few bones there and blood fucking everywhere. I reasoned that if a person died before turning or without being infected the deedaz must feast on it until there's nothing left. Then I reasoned to stop fucking reasoning and hurry the fuck up.

 I made it to the bottle neck and ran between the houses to the trees and stupidly risked a look behind me. The zombies had followed at a... I can't say run exactly, but they certainly weren't walking. If I could describe it I'd say lauping. Is that a word? Imagine Dr Frankenstein's assistant, Igor, trying to run. Sort of like that. Not fast but enough to put the shits right up you.

As I breached the trees the enormity of what had happened to the world unfolded before my eyes. The road was packed with abandoned cars as far as the eye could see. All four lanes in both directions. Body parts covered in flies lay everywhere. Scattered throughout the mayhem and standing staring at me were the walking dead. Again with the fucking moaning.

I bounded on to the roof of the car I was nearest to, sending up a black swathe of flies and prepared to play the world's most dangerous game of frogger. Luckily the cars I planned on using to cross the road to hell were lined up perfectly but looked slick with the offal the flies had left behind.

Frozen by indecision, a hand grasped the back of my trouser leg. Instinct took over and I leapt for the next car, pulling free of the hand that had ensnared me.

I've always thought I was quite a bright chap. I was quite well educated and understood the basics of most things in life. Science being one of them, although I failed to remember the principles of gravity and the fact I was carrying a big fuck-off rucksack.

I slammed into the car I was jumping for like a fat lass opening a chip shop door.

Stunned and lying between the cars in amongst the gore of my fellow man I quickly scrambled to my feet and surveyed my options. All of the cars I could see were bumper to bumper, most of them fender benders, so wiggling my way between them was out of the question. My exits were cut off by deedaz converging towards me along the aisles the cars made. I hefted myself up on to the car I'd slammed into and jumped down on to the grass verge between the opposing carriageways. A short hop over the knee-high safety barrier and I was halfway there. This side of the road had some spaces between the bumpers of the multitude of cars so I weaved through and finally found myself facing an open fenced field. The field ran adjacent to the road for a least a mile, but if I simply walked through it, parallel to the road, I would be seen by every deeda along the gridlocked highway.

On the far side of the field was a wood which I knew to be quite large. It separated my town and my ex's town and had a river that dissected it from west to east.

I'd spent a lot of time in those woods when I was younger, but mostly on the north side, which had a beautiful, well-walked country path that followed the waterway all the way to the North Sea. I had explored the south side a little in my youth. I used to go there when I was in my early teens with my best friend Joey Davis. We'd spend the day there whenever we skived from school. The perfect place for dodging any of the many truant officers that patrolled the streets of Northumberland.

There were no paths to speak of. The odd fox or deer track could be found, but apart from that there were no discernible routes, though the likelihood of bumping in to a deeda on the south side was far less than travelling the northern side's route.

I made my way over the field towards the woods. As I was about to enter the shaded canopy of trees I turned to check behind me towards the main road I'd crossed. The fence I'd just climbed over was now home to a group of around fifteen deedaz. I was spurred into continuing my journey when one of them fell over the barbed wire fence and into the field.

Chapter 17 – The nest

Once into trees I headed east, next to the meandering river. I did see the odd deeda on the opposite bank but thankfully nothing at all on the side I was on. The next few hours were really hard going. More or less cutting my own path through the undergrowth, fully aware that the deeda that fell over the fence may not be too far behind. Having to stop and listen after every step started to take its toll and after what felt like ten miles (it was actually about two) I had to take a rest. It was now late afternoon and with no solid structures to be found and night only a few hours away I had to come up with a plan so I could rest safely.

I took out some paracord, tied it to the handle of my rucksack and climbed a huge old tree I'd came across. Once up to the crook of the tree, which was around ten feet from the ground, I hauled my rucksack up with me. After digging around in the sack I took out my paracord hammock and tied it across the two main limbs about fifteen feet from the ground. Bed sorted I went about securing my sack to the tree and sat and ate one of the MREs (an army acronym for Meals Ready to Eat) from my bugout bag. With no option to eat it other than cold I wolfed it down with gusto. So much better than the noodles and soup I'd been living on for the past month. Chilli with rice with an orange drink, finished off with chocolate biscuits.

Now loaded with calories I pulled out my sleeping bag and inserted it into the bivi bag. The chance of rain was small but when dawn came round, the morning dew would most likely dampen the sleeping bag by itself. I decided to get into the hammock before it started getting dark. Anyone who has ever tried to mount a hammock will know how hard it is to do. Never mind fifteen feet from the ground. I had practised with it when I'd first bought said item and after a good few hours I'd perfected the technique. Although I forgot to practise how I'd get into the sleeping bag once I'd got in, never mind doing all this at altitude.

I hung the bag over the supporting rope of the hammock nearest where my head would be. Carefully and not very gracefully I settled into my temporary string bed and slowly wormed myself into the sleeping/bivi bag. It took almost fifteen minutes but I didn't mind. I felt relatively safe up there.

Before I fell asleep I reflected on the day I'd had. My escape from the loft, the poor waif trapped in her house with her deeda husband, her awful demise, my inability to come to her aid and the gauntlet I had run through the estate and carriageway. Maybe the future would be better. Maybe by this time tomorrow I'd be sailing away from all of this terror.

Maybe I'd find an island and live happily ever after. Maybe.

I was not looking forward to falling asleep that night, as the events of the previous day would no doubt have a profound effect on my dreams. I reasoned my subconscious mind would punish me through the medium of dream for being so indecisive.

Guilt is a terrible thing to live with, especially when people have died by your hand. Well, not by my hand personally, but you know what I mean. I could have warned Max to stay away from the old man who had bitten him. On reflection, I truly didn't know or expect the old man to be an actual zombie but I did have the information I'd learned from the TV on that fateful morning and probably should have told him all that I knew when he asked, instead of telling him a pack of lies about riots and terrorists. Maybe he would still be alive. In all likelihood, he would have laughed at me and run to the old man's aid anyway. Alice, of course, was beyond help. There was no way I could have helped her without being torn apart myself. Maybe I could have distracted them by shouting out of the window and drawing them to me. I doubt they'd have come when the chance of a meal was only a broomstick away. And as for Skeletor, I could have passed up the food I'd had in the bugout bag but never could I have guessed that she'd react the way she did. It was over in seconds.

There was nothing I could have done to save her.

As I lay there under a canopy of green and brown pondering my actions, I concluded that there was nothing I could do about anything that had happened since the deedaz had arrived. I couldn't change anything. There was no use debating shoulda, woulda, coulda. All I could do was take each day as it came and hope that my future decision making would be more decisive and definitely more proactive. As the night drew in and with the hammock gently swinging, thoughts turned to my ex. I still loved her terribly and if I could go back and change the way I had been I would have. To be honest I was worried sick about her, but we hadn't been in touch for what seemed like a life time. I toyed with the idea of detouring into her town to see if she needed help but dismissed the notion. I don't think I'd cope if she'd been turned, even more so if I arrived and he was there protecting her from the zombie masses with his fucking pecs. Okay, I am bitter!

Eventually I drifted off into a deep dreamless sleep.

Chapter 18 – The rude awakening

I awoke with a jolt at dawn. As if smelling salts had been placed directly under my nose. I'd experienced this feeling before when I was in middle school.

I was one of the youngest in my class, hence one of the smallest. Never being any good at sports I was somehow elected as house captain. It was purely a popularity vote and had nothing to do with my sporting prowess. This fact didn't endear me to the teacher who was house leader, and he reminded me at every opportunity that the choice made by my peers in electing me was the wrong one.

The smelling salts incident happened on the final sports day of the last year before going to high school. As I mentioned before, I wasn't any good at sports so imagine my surprise when I found my name on the rugby team sheet. WTF? After ten minutes of remonstrating to the evil twat of a teacher that not only did I not know the rules of said sport, I was also fucking tiny compared with the rest of the team. The majority of them sported bum fluff beards and protruding Adam's apples. At the time I had just entered into the realms of puberty and possessed a very unreliable voice and two pubes.

As expected, my rugby experience wasn't pleasant and within the first three minutes of the game I received the gift of a serious concussion, a broken arm and a nose full of smelling salts. The teacher had won. Wanker.

These memories came flooding back as I lay there in my hammock and felt a phantom ache in the arm I'd broken. Awareness of my surroundings broke through my temporary walk down memory lane. The sun was beginning to rise as I peered over the side of the hammock and down to the forest floor. As soon as I did so, the moaning started. There were three of them. Stinking deedaz. They were dry so they hadn't traversed the river. They had to be the ones that followed me from the highway. I must have been snoring during the night and they'd zeroed in on me. The moaning soon stopped when I lay back down, but they didn't move away. I had two choices, stay where I was and hope that they eventually left or get in amongst it and go Chuck Norris on the fuckers. I decided to stay where I was and hoped they left. What can I say. At the time I was obviously a coward. It was evident. It had been six weeks and all I'd done was run and hide. I'd been lucky enough that I'd never had to properly defend myself against one of them and I wasn't about to start now.

Three hours passed and the burning sensation in my bladder was starting to become a problem. I have my routine, you see, and this wasn't it. The deedaz were still down there and hadn't moved an inch. I'd hoped something in the woods might have lured them away. A fox, a bird. Anything. Nothing came to my rescue with a diversion. Only one thing for it. I unzipped the sleeping bag and inched the bivi bag down to my waist, shuffled onto my side and emptied my bladder all over the fuckers. This sent them into an absolute frenzy. Either they were really upset that I was pissing on them or somehow they knew warm piss meant warm food. Their moans echoed through the forest and were answered with other distant moans. Shit.

Spurred in to action I climbed out of the hammock and sat in the crook of the tree. It was large enough that it obscured their view of me and the moaning soon stopped, as did the distant moaning.

The time to step up and be the person I thought I'd be, had come. I had to get the fuck out of dodge again. Back in the loft I'd had the foresight to bring some of the pund chunks from the loose change jar for this very reason. I took one out of the bugout bag. Before I threw it, I unhooked my machete and hatchet and looped the lanyards of both around my wrists. The plan was to distract them with the money, jump down and windmill into the horrible bastards. Not the best plan, I admit, but the only one I could think of. The drop from the lowest branch was only around eight feet and the ground was soft with debris. If I didn't break my ankle in the process I had a fighting chance. The deedaz would be facing away from me so I could hopefully weigh into them before they knew what was happening.

With a flick of my wrist the coin flew straight and true and clattered off the trunk of a tree a short distance away. As expected the dead were pulled away from my tree in search of the sound. The moaning started again, as did the distant moaning.

I summoned every ounce of courage, which, if you could actually weigh courage, would have probably only weighed about an ounce, and dropped down onto the forest floor.

They all turned towards me simultaneously. FUCK! So glad I'd had that piss. I'd be doing the backstroke if I hadn't.

My mind went into overdrive. Fight or flight. If I ran I'd be running away from my bugout bag. At least I was down from that tree and not trapped anymore. So there I was. In a small clearing, in a forest, dressed in a camo onesie, loaded for bear with a weapon in each hand and three zombie mother fuckers twelve feet away from me. I ran away. You knew I would. But I didn't run far. It was all part of plan B.

The zombies 'lauped' after me but, being zombies and having limited locomotive skills, they soon tripped on the various roots and branches on the forest floor. This was the opportunity I had planned for. With the hatchet in my right hand I retraced my steps and slammed the pointy end smack in the top of the first zombie I came to. It was a man dressed in a two-piece suit with a single bite on the right side of his face. His skin was battleship grey and his lips were a deep purple. Good name for a band that.

I was surprised how easily the axe penetrated the skull. This could have been the adrenaline making me super strong or because of decomposition. I opted for the first reason. Mainly because of the confidence it gave me for my upcoming battle royal with the other two deedaz. With a gut-churning slurp, I removed the gore-covered axe from its head and stalked up to my next target.

This one was nearly up on his feet. As I approached he lunged at me, teeth gnashing. I quickly side stepped what was left of its mauled, grasping hands and sliced down left handed with the machete on the back of its neck. To my surprise its head came clean off. I felt like the fucking Hulk!

The confidence that flowed through me nearly became the end of me. As I stood triumphantly over the headless corpse, the final deeda thought it a good time to introduce itself. This one was a woman and a big fucker she was too. She came up from behind and grabbed my right arm and went in for a bite. If I hadn't screamed like a girl and pulled away she'd have bitten me. She still gripped my arm as I started running around in a circle, with her in the centre, trying to knock her off balance. I did the first thing that came to mind. Still believing I had superpowers I imagined a hefty swipe with machete would slice clean through the fat fuck's arm. I found out, in pure shock, that I didn't have super powers after all. The machete sliced through her bingo wings and stopped at the bone. I withdrew the machete and hacked away at her arm while still doing the Morris dance from hell. The bone was just too strong. Fat lasses must really be just big boned after all.

Then it dawned on me what to do. I placed the sharp side of the machete on the underside of her wrist that held me and drew it across with as much strength as I could muster. The grip on my arm relinquished immediately as I cut through the tendons. Without having me there to lean on, she stumbled forward and fell face first into the nearest tree. With a crunch, she lay there unmoving except for the still chomping teeth. She must have broken her neck when she'd face planted the sturdy trunk. I didn't have the stomach to finish her off and couldn't face the dry heaving that would surely follow. With the adrenaline well and truly out of my system I made my way back to my tree to recover my possessions. I had to do this quickly. The noise I'd just made despatching the three stooges must have attracted the deedaz I'd heard earlier, as I could hear the breaking of twigs and branches coming from the direction I'd travelled from the day before.

Stuffing the hammock and sleeping bag in the rucksack it dawned on me that I could have used my crossbow to end the fuckers from the safety of my tree. What a fuckwit.

Chapter 19 – The loner

I strapped on the bag and headed east towards the sea, immensely proud of myself and feeling a lot more confident in my abilities.

Following the river on this side would eventually bring me to the seaside town of Blyth.

Blyth is one of the other large towns in Northumberland so would obviously be full of the infected, but it did have a harbour and would surely have boats there. On the other side of the river opposite Blyth was a little place called North Blyth, which was really just a dozen rows of terraced houses and was literally cut off from 'big' Blyth in the late eighties when the ferry that joined the two stopped running. Now the residents of North Blyth had a tenmile drive via the nearest bridge to get into Blyth itself. To the north of North Blyth was a place called Cambois, pronounced cammis. Don't really know the origins of the name. It sounds French. I'd google it if I could.

Anyway, Cambois was really just a long street with a row of terraced houses on one side, overlooking the road and facing the sea. It used to be home to the local power station but that was demolished a few years ago. I knew that two miles north of Cambois, at the mouth of the estuary of the River Wansbeck, was a little boatyard that was home to numerous fishing boats. Maybe I could find something there.

It was further away than the harbour at Blyth but wasn't nearly as populated as the large town would be.

After a three-hour trudge, still stopping and listening with every step I took, I navigated my way over a road that led to the ex's town, and continued on, cutting my way through the overgrown south side. Eventually, at around noon, I came out of the woods into bright sunshine and crossed a single-lane bridge and made my way towards Cambois, now travelling on the north side of the river. This was the stretch of the journey I wasn't looking forward to. The path next to the river ran parallel to a road that was situated on the outskirts of a place called Bedlington Station. Though the road was a good thirty meters away and was separated from the path by bushes and a slight incline, I still felt, for the first time since leaving my housing estate, that I was rather exposed and hemmed in. I knew if I had to, I could probably jump the fence and make an escape through the river, but being close to the sea now meant the river had widened considerably and the mud flats would be a dangerous obstacle whether the tide was in or out.

Suddenly on the path in front of me a deeda stumbled out of the undergrowth and stopped. Luckily it faced away from me but unluckily it was blocking the only route I could take. Why had he moved onto the path in the first place? Had he heard me coming? I had been walking as stealthily as I could, but the with the path being gravel it was virtually impossible not to make some kind of sound.

If he had heard me coming, why was he facing away from me? Something else must have piqued his interest.

What was I going to do? I couldn't go back. I couldn't detour without having to travel through quite a big built-up area and the river option was only for extreme emergencies.

I'd have to fucking kill it. I was a little more confident in my abilities after the showdown I'd had that morning with the three deedaz that gave me my early morning wake up call. The first two were easy and even though the big fat mamma nearly got the best of me, I had thought on my feet, stayed relatively calm and triumphed.

I had three choices.

1. I could go in running, catch it by surprise and finish it quickly, then be on my way.
2. I could go all ninja on the mutha fucker and stealth kill it.
3. I could distract it with the pund chunk trick and sneak past it.

Each choice had negative points to take into consideration.

Choice one would get noisy and definitely attract more of the scary bastards towards my vicinity.

Choice two would mean I'd have to get close to it without it hearing me before I could deliver the ending strike.

Choice three would probably cost me a fucking fortune.

I decided that this time discretion was in order. Ninja time!

Next to the path was a six-inch wide swathe of grass and weeds that ran alongside. I would use this to disguise the sound of my footsteps on the gravel path. The filthy bastard was, at the most, thirty feet away. Carefully and silently I stalked down the walkway in one hand my hatchet and in the other, my crossbow pistol. Finally I was going to get to use it. When I was around ten feet away I stopped and lined the sights of the crossbow with the back of the deedaz' head. All of a sudden the deedaz' head started to tilt backwards. What was he doing? Was there something in the sky drawing his attention? A bird, or better still a rescue helicopter. I started scanning the sky too, in hope it was someone coming to my salvation.

Then it dawned on me. He wasn't looking at anything. He was sniffing. That was the reason he'd moved out of the bushes. He'd gotten a whiff of me then lost the scent.

The deeda spun round towards me when he'd pinpointed the direction the scent had come from. How could I have forgotten the smell thing, after I'd gone to all that trouble retrieving the money jar to test out the deedaz' abilities?

In a panic, I squeezed the trigger on the crossbow at exactly the same time the zombie had started to lunge and moan. To my utter amazement the bolt flew out of the crossbow and into the right eye of the deeda. It slumped to the floor like a puppet with its strings cut. The whole event was over in seconds without a noise being made. Well, apart from the twang of the crossbow, but that was minimal and I was sure it hadn't been heard. He could keep the bolt. There was no way I was plucking that out. I couldn't bear the thought that it could pop out with the eyeball attached. I had another forty-nine bolts in my rucksack anyway. I just hoped I'd never regret not taking it back one day.

I travelled on, counting my lucky stars and thanking whoever was looking out for me. I just hoped my luck would last until I reached the boatyard.

Chapter 20 – The flying dead

Before long I had to pass under the bridged main road that ran north to south and connected many of the towns along the northern coastline. It was aptly named the spine road and from what I could see, it was total gridlock. It was also packed with deedaz. As I approached it from beside the river I was spotted by one of them. Then the moans went up and more of them began to crowd the fence overlooking me. I wasn't too worried about this because the bridge was around seventy feet high. I quickened my pace and knew once out of sight they would calm and stop making such a fucking racket.

Never in a million years did I think it would start raining fucking zombies. The first one missed me by inches. I jumped back and another splattered on top of it. I looked up and another five were on their way down. I ran as fast as I could and prepared to leap over the first two zombies that had fallen, completely forgetting Sir Isaac Newton's laws of gravity again. Big rucksack = no jumpy jumpy.

My leading foot clipped the top zombie and I went arse over tit, gaining a face full of gravel as my reward for being such a stupid fuck. I'd learn eventually.

Shocked and dazed I crawled away from the rising pile of deedaz behind me and chanced a glance back toward them. I wish I hadn't. Three of them had survived the fall and we're crawling towards me. I'd finally gained control of my bladder now, so thankfully didn't add to the river running at my side. Amazingly, apart from the gravel in my face, I wasn't injured in any way, so I scrambled to my feet and ran as fast as I could.

I knew now I had to head north and parallel to the spine road. There was a small tributary that filtered into the river further along and no way of getting across it if I kept going east. Throwing myself over a fence I travelled north through a farmer's field, traversing beside a thick hedge which thankfully hid me from any milky dead eyes that may have spotted me from the spine road.

Finally I came to the small bridge I'd have to use. I'd be stepping out of the safety of the field but there was no other way across.

At this point I'd realised that I'd never seen another living person since I'd left the culde-sac. How could the majority of the country have been affected this way? The only reason that I could fathom was family. Again, I was lucky in this situation because I had none. Imagine, you're sitting having a cup of tea and your wife/husband comes in looking decidedly drunk and injured. You wouldn't run. You'd go straight to them to help or give them shit for being drunk so early in the day. Then you're one of them. As simple as that. If I hadn't had that bout of insomnia on that fateful night, I too would have been outside with Max watching the helicopter and I'd have run to the aid of the old man. Maybe.

The resulting exodus of people trying to escape in their cars was the final nail in the coffin. Where did they expect to go to? Nowhere on this tiny island we live on is safe, and even if you did think of somewhere, the probability that a thousand more people had thought of the same place was too great. It dawned on me that my plan had most probably been thought of too. My heart sank. If I got to the boatyard and there was nothing to get me out to sea I'd be fucked. Proper fucked.

I'd put all of my eggs in one basket with this plan of mine. Well, you never know until you try. I'd have to cross that metaphorical bridge when I came to it. In the meantime, I had to cross the very real bridge in front of me first.

All I needed to do was slip on to the path that ran along the side of the road, scoot over the bridge then back into the fields and follow the tributary towards the coast, cut across the old power station grounds and make my way to the beach. From there north to the boatyard. Piece of piss.

Chapter 21 – The hero

No sooner had I stepped on to the bridge than I heard a sound I hadn't heard in what felt like years. The sound of a large engine coming from behind me and travelling my way. My first thought was to hide from it. Too many zombie novels and films I'm afraid. In every one I've read or watched it turns out that other humans are probably more dangerous than the dead. Then I realised this was the UK not a fucking Mad Max film. I stood and waited for the vehicle to emerge from the bend. The tractor that came in to view was the last thing I'd expected. What I had expected was some armoured, scrapheap-challenge, apocalyptic shit with sculls on the bonnet driven by a leather-clad warrior with a pink Mohican. Then I remembered. This was not Mad fucking Max.

The driver drove past, gave me a glance, then turned back to driving the behemoth of a tractor. Something must have registered in the driver because he slammed his brakes on bringing the tractor to a shuddering halt and turned off the engine. He slowly turned in his seat and looked straight at me. Opening the door, he leaned out and said, 'Fuck me, are you alive?'

'Just,' I answered.

'Well hurry the fuck up and climb in before the stinkaz get here.'

That was it. Twelve words and I turned into a blubbering mess. For some reason my legs went from under me and I ended up on my knees, hands on the ground, sobbing uncontrollably. If he'd put his tractor into gear and trundled off into the sunset I wouldn't have blamed him. There I was, on all fours, dressed in a piss and gore stained camo onesie and crying like a mackem at the end of the season. I'd never realised that my mental state had deteriorated so much over the past weeks of solitude. To finally see someone else alive and not at death's door was utterly overwhelming.

The words, 'What the fucks wrong with you?' brought me to my senses.

I clambered to my feet and jogged over to the tractor while wiping the tears and snot on the sleeve of my onesie.

'Sorry mate, I thought I was the only person left,' I explained.

'Well, hurry the fuck up and climb in. The stinkaz are coming.'

I turned towards the direction he'd come from and sure enough, an army of approximately a hundred deedaz were coming our way.

'I'm like the fucking pied piper with this thing,' he said, gesturing towards the tractor with a nod.

I climbed in, shut the door and sat in the seat next to him. Without a word he just smiled, started the engine and drove onward.

I introduced myself and shook his shovel like hand as I thanked him for picking me up.

'Not a problem,' he said. 'You're the first live person I've seen in weeks too.'

He told me his name was Darren and he lived and worked on his father's farm a few miles away. Darren was bald and at a guess was around the same age as me. With very broad shoulders, he unsurprisingly owned the complexion of someone who spent their lives outdoors. Rugged and definitely not to be trifled with. He'd been holed up at the farm until that morning.

Darren had also seen the news reports on the night the world changed. Being a farmer, getting up before dawn every day was the norm and he'd caught the tail end of the chaos on the news as he made breakfast.

My saviour admitted he too was a bit of a prepper and went about fortifying the farmhouse he lived in. All of the downstairs windows were promptly boarded up and his trusty tractor was parked beneath the porch at the front of his home. At no point did he mention the fate of his father, which I thought was a little strange, so instead I planned to enquire about this when I got to know him a little better.

The decision to leave the security of his homestead was made for him when the house had been unexplainably surrounded by the 'stinkaz', as he liked to call them.

He'd waited until they had breached the back door before he fled. Climbing out of the upstairs window and onto the top of the porch, he climbed down onto the tractor's roof and lowered himself inside.

The crowd of stinkaz that had gathered never stood a chance against the might of the brand new John Deere tractor. It had trampled the dead with no effort at all. It was then I noticed that there were indeed the remnants of deedaz in the grooves of the vehicle's very large tyres.

'Where are you headed?' I asked. To my surprise Darren had had the exact same plan as me. He was heading for the boatyard. I was starting to like this guy.

The only thing I didn't like was the noise the tractor created.

The next mile of travel turned out to be uneventful. We'd passed a couple of shambler deedaz and the odd crawly one and thought the journey to the boatyard was going to be continue to be uneventful. That is until we turned onto the main street that ran through Cambois.

For some unexplained reason it was full of the dead, most of them gathered around one house in particular. There was a small council estate around three-quarters of a mile away so I could only guess that the majority of the deedaz were from there. The smell that blew through the cab of the tractor was horrendous.

I turned to look at Darren and was bemused to why he was smiling a devilish grin. It was when he started revving the tractor engine that I realised his intentions. 'Let me show you what this baby can do,' he shouted.

At the sound of the engine revving the dead turned as one and converged on the tractor. Without a moment's hesitation Darren floored it. You're probably thinking 'floor a tractor?' Well, apparently you can. We shot off towards the oncoming deedaz and carved a path through them like a hot knife through butter. With hardly a shudder from the multitudes of bodies it crushed it ploughed on and past the house the deedaz had congregated around.

There, in the upstairs window of the house, was a rather large, barking dog. How long it had been up there attracting the dead was anyone's guess. The deedaz in the street below had obviously been unable to gain access to the heavily barricaded front door and windows. I was pretty sure whoever secured the house were not there to restrain the dog from barking. Then that left the question of how was the dog still alive without owners to feed it. Unless it was feeding on its owners? I pushed that gruesome thought from my head and concentrated on the gruesome panorama in front of me.

I turned to Darren and was reminded of a scene from the movie *Planes, trains and automobiles*. He really did look like the laughing devil as he annihilated the dead with his motorised hound of hell. The windscreen wiper moved at full belt, smearing the gore and detritus of the dead over the glass. Finally we broke through and continued north to our hoped-for salvation.

The boatyard was only around two miles away, but with most of the dead that had avoided the wheels of the tractor following us at a 'laup' we'd only have around thirty minutes to find and launch something that could float.

The road that we entered to access the boatyard was home to a pub and a few converted barns. I'd ashamedly hoped that the residents here were either dead or had escaped using other forms of transport. My whole plan hinged on getting on the water. The only other accessible harbour I knew of was approximately twenty miles north in a place called Amble and would surely have scores of the dead there.

Chapter 22 – The lucky shot

We passed the pub without any drama and trundled along the lane. The gates to the boatyard lay ahead, but there were five deedaz standing in wait in front of them who seemed intent on getting to something inside the secure yard. I was surprised at the fact they hadn't turned and assaulted the tractor. I didn't take long to see why. Directly on the other side of the fence a man was trying unsuccessfully to drag a small fishing boat across the yard. Behind the boat was a young girl of around eighteen pushing with everything she had. They obviously hadn't heard the tractor because of the effort of trying to move the boat. That and the moaning from the dead at the gate must have muffled the sound the engine made. Until Darren beeped the horn, that is.

The couple stopped their impossible task and looked our way. They didn't seem too glad to see us. I know this because in a flash the man drew what looked like a shotgun and pointed it towards us.

'Don't worry,' Darren said. 'He hasn't got a clean shot with all those stinkaz in the way and we're too far away for a shotgun to do any real harm.'

This revelation did nothing to make me feel any better. A gun's a gun's a gun.

Darren opened the glass door of the cab and leaned out. 'No need for the hostilities friend. You look like you need a tow and we need a boat, and that tub looks big enough for us all. Also, there's around over a hundred stinkaz on their way from Cambois that will arrive in about twenty minutes. You need us, we need you.'

To say I was impressed with the calmness and bravery Darren showed would be an understatement and I started to thank the heavens that I'd met him.

Shotgun-man lowered the gun and seemed to be having a conversation with the young girl behind the boat.

'OK, but I can't open the gate with the dead there,' he shouted.

Darren looked at me with another one of his devilish grins. 'What?' I asked.

'Time to get those blades dirty' he said as he lifted what looked like two small sledgehammers with both hands. Without another word he deftly leapt from the tractor door and stood gesturing me to follow. Not wanting to look like a proper softie I jumped down beside him.

The deedaz now seeing an easier meal standing in front of them advanced on us.

Of the five dead, two of them were of the walker ilk. The other three were definite 'Igors'. Luckily for me, two of them went straight for Darren. My respect for him increased to god like when I saw how he despatched the deedaz. With one fell swoop he lifted both hammers above his head and simultaneously brought them down on both of the deedaz heads. They both fell in heaps at his feet with very sizeable divots in their melons.

With awe I watched as he put one foot triumphantly onto a deeda and held one of his hammers aloft, Thor-like.

That more than likely would have been the last thing I ever saw if the god of thunder hadn't looked at me and thrown his lofted hammer in my direction. In shock I followed the hammer as it came towards me, spinning through the air. This all happened so fast all I could do was close my eyes and wait for death. Instead, I heard a thump and a crack. Slowly I opened my eyes and saw the third lauping deeda at my feet. Somehow Darren had calculated his throw to where he knew the deeda would be when it hit. He'd saved my life.

Who the fuck was this guy?

As I stood rooted to the spot he smiled and calmly walked to the two deedaz that were left and despatched them with the ease of swatting flies.

I retrieved his hammer from the cranium of the fucker that nearly ended me and walked over to Darren.

'Fucking hell, thanks mate,' I said. 'Nee botha pal,' was his reply. 'Let's go and see this fuckwit with the gun.'

Darren walked up to the gate where the man was unlooping a chain that held it closed.

'The names Darren, this is my friend Carter. Thanks for not shooting us.'

'Thanks for getting rid of the zeds,' the man said. 'My name is Andy, this is my daughter Bobby.' With the pleasantries out of the way, Andy asked Darren, 'Where the fuck did you learn to do that shit anyway?'

'What shit?' Darren asked innocently.

'The fucking ninja turtle shit you just did on the zeds.'

'Oh, that shit. Just saw what needed to be done and did it. Lucky shot when I threw the hammer I guess.'

'Lucky shot my arse,' I thought. There was no way any normal person would have risked a shot like that. A normal person would have pointed and shouted 'Look out!' We stood there looking at each other. Darren obviously wasn't going to elaborate on his talent for killing 'zeds' so I interrupted the awkward silence and reminded everyone that a flock of deedaz were still on the way.

Chapter 23 – The open sea

After Darren drove the tractor through the gate, Andy secured it again with the length of chain. Five minutes later Darren had hooked up the boat and deftly reversed into the waterway that led to the sea.

Seemingly from nowhere Andy and Bobby started heaving bottled water and what looked like boxes of food from a shipping container into the boat.

'Where'd you get all that from?' I asked.

'We've been planning this for a few weeks,' Andy explained. 'I've been making runs down here for the past few days. We owned a shop in Stakeford before all this happened.'

I knew Stakeford quite well. Not really a village or a town. More like a borough that was on the outskirts of another large town called Ashington. My grandparents used to live there and I knew the shop he owned. It was a small local supermarket.

'On our last run our pickup ran out of petrol about a mile away. I'd been planning on moving the boat with it but I'd syphoned half of the tank and put it in the boat. In hindsight,

I should have moved the boat first.'

I helped Andy and Bobby to load the rest of the provisions into the boat while 'Thor' guarded the gate. Just as the last box was aboard Darren shouted, 'They're here!' Without a word between us we climbed into the boat and started the engine. Darren bounded over from the gates carrying a rather large rucksack on his back, another in his hand, and what looked to be some kind of case for an electric guitar. He didn't strike me as the musician type and I couldn't think of any situation we'd ever be in for him to break out in song. But hey, he'd just saved my life. Twice. Who was I to stop him if he wanted to strum out 'I've got a brand new combine harvester'? I'd put some fucking harmonies on if it meant he'd keep throwing those fucking hammers to save my arse.

The boat itself was nothing to write home about. It was eighteen feet long, had no cabin but had quite a large outboard motor.

As we pulled away from the boatyard the gate gave way to the multitude of deedaz that had arrived. They Igored down the ramp towards the waterway and stopped as they came to the water's edge. With a collective mournful wail they watched as their warm meal chugged away towards the sea and freedom.

'Where to?' Asked Andy as he steered us out of the waterway and out to sea.

'North is our best bet,' replied Darren.
Bobby, who until that moment hadn't said anything, chirped up with, 'Why north?'

Darren went on to explain the whys and wherefores and it turned out he thought exactly the same as I did.

Northumberland as a whole had a relatively small population and with us living in the south of the county the farther north you went the towns got smaller and more distant from each other. Also peppered along the coast were a group bird sanctuaries called the Farne Islands which happened to have buildings on them for the wildlife wardens who lived there.
The perfect place to ride out this apocalyptic storm.

All we had to do was get there.

As we turned north out of the waterway a new chorus of moans greeted us from the beach. The beach belonged to a caravan park that sat above the sand dunes. Sandy Bay caravan park to be exact. I know this because I'd sung there a couple of times over the years. Ironic really because now the holiday makers were serenading me.

Deedaz of all ages crowded the beach, reaching out toward us. It was the first time I'd seen child deedaz and hoped it would be the last. It was heartbreaking to see the damage they had taken, most likely from one of their own family.

'They're not going anywhere near the water,' Bobby noticed.

She was right, the deedaz were standing right on the tide line of the beach and it looked like they definitely had no intention of getting their feet wet. This bode well for all of us. Andy decided to take us further out to sea because the throng of dead started following the boat along the beach. I was definitely apprehensive about this and although the sea was being kind to us by not being too choppy, the biggest worry was running out of fuel or having mechanical problems and being at the mercy of the unforgiving North Sea, which I knew could be a right twat if it wanted to be.

After a while the dead on the beach gave up the chase. It would take about an hour and a half to reach our destination and we all sat in silence contemplating our future and praying our salvation was just up the coast. Andy made use of the lull in conversation to apologise about pointing the gun at us when we arrived and added the fact that it didn't actually work. He'd bought it from an antique shop years ago and had intended to use it as an ornament to hang it above the fireplace. The firing pin had been filed down and rendered the firearm unusable.

 I later found out from Bobby that word had gotten out around the Stakeford area that Andy owned the shotgun and an 'urban myth' was born that the local kids believed to be true: 'Steal from Andy and he'll shoot ye'. The parents in the area would fuel the myth in the hope their children would not stay the straight and narrow. Andy became the legendary 'Shotgun Andy' and never ever came up short on stock taking day.

Chapter 24 – The welcome party

We soon came upon the first island we'd planned to scope out. Coquet Island.

With an area of around fifteen acres and home to a lighthouse and outbuildings, and around half a mile from the coastal town of Amble, we had all agreed this would be an ideal place of sanctuary if it was uninhabited.

The island loomed larger as we approached, and Bobby suddenly proclaimed from her vantage point at the front of the boat, 'People!'

I moved next to her for a closer view. She was right. In the distance on the small beach of the island were a group of around fifteen to twenty people. And it looked like they needed help and were trying to get our attention.

Andy steered the boat towards the beach but brought it to a stop when we all realised the people there were past help. They were dead.

Fuck!

'What will we do now dad?' Bobby asked. Andy didn't say a word. He just shook his head.

I looked at Darren and shrugged. 'Well, we'll just have to go find another island.'

Darren sat there passively and obviously in thought. To him, the island was too good to give up on. From our viewpoint the lighthouse and obvious living accommodation looked like a fortress. The island could only be accessed from the small beach and a small jetty. The rest of the perimeter of the island consisted of sheer cliffs. This place was perfect.

With another one of his devilish grins he announced, 'I've got an idea'.

As far as ideas go, I must admit it was a good one. Although we'd all be putting ourselves within reach of the dead, my faith in Darren exceeded any thoughts of chickening out. He was fast becoming the leader of our merry little band and I for one was glad of it.
Nothing seemed to phase or frighten the guy. He was absolutely solid.

The plan was to circle the island in the boat within view of the deedaz and hopefully get them to follow. This, in effect, would spread them out, making it easier for us to get ashore and dish out some zombie head caving one on one.

Andy steered north between the Northumbrian coast and Coquet Island, and planned to navigate around it in a clockwise direction. The deedaz followed en masse up along the beach and along the cement jetty that jutted out to sea. Bobby shouted, 'It's not working, they're all coming along the pier thingy. We need them spread out around the island. We need to turn around and go the other way.'

Again, I looked at Darren. Again with the grin. I glanced back at the pier and it dawned on me exactly what was going to happen.

The deedaz at the front eventually made it to the end of the pier and stopped. But the slower deedaz behind them frantically tried to push their way to the front of the queue an, in doing so, toppled their brethren into the crashing sea. This practically halved their numbers.

'Turn it round and head for the beach Andy,' Darren shouted. 'And give it some gas, we all need to get off and sort out the fuckers that are left, and the boat needs to be partly beached so it doesn't float away.'

Andy then told Darren in no uncertain terms that no way was Bobby getting on that island until the deedaz were dealt with.

'Can Bobby drive this boat if it floats back out to sea Andy?' Darren asked.

Andy said nothing, knowing that she couldn't.

'Well put your fucking foot down and beach the fucking boat mate.'

Andy did as instructed and with an enormous scraping sound the boat landed on the beach and came to a stop. Before Andy had switched off the engine Darren had hopped over the side of the boat and stormed the beach like it was fucking Normandy.

Now in full-on berserker mode, Darren went to work. The faster deedaz that hadn't been pushed into the sea had reached the beach and had the pleasure of meeting Darren first.

In his previous life candidate number one looked to have been a fisherman of some kind, judging by his attire. The large rubber wader pants and hi-vis jacket under a life vest were a dead giveaway.

It came within reach of Darren and was about to grab him when Darren ducked under the outstretched arms and swung one of his hammers at the deedaz knee. The knee snapped with a horrible crack and the deeda went down in a heap. Not a killing move but definitely immobilised.

Without stopping Darren literally windmilled into the trailing deedaz that were left and shouted over his shoulder, 'Carter, mop the fuck up son.'

I immediately came out of my reverie and realised I was still on the boat. I practically fell over the side and ran through the surf up onto the beach with my bolo and hatchet drawn and commenced the gruesome job of ending the incapacitated deedaz that squirmed in the trail of destruction that Darren had left in his wake. 'Who the fuck is this guy?' I asked myself. Again.

He was like Woody Harrelson's character, Tallahassee, from *Zombieland*. On fucking steroids! Not one foot did he put wrong, the hammers in his hands swinging and arcing in a glorious ballet of blood and brains. One would think the spectacle I was viewing had been choreographed and rehearsed. Within a few minutes it was over and Darren walked back toward us, blood dripping from his hammers. Hammers which had absolutely been blessed by Odin himself.

'What the fucking fuck mate,' I said. 'Who the fuck are you?'

'Just your friendly local farmer,' he said laughingly. 'Listen, we'll talk later, first we need to check this island out and secure those buildings. Andy, anchor the boat and stay with Bobby. We're going to check the lighthouse.'

Chapter 25 – The haven

Darren and I carefully stalked up the path that led up to the lighthouse. In the field next to the buildings was a small group of fifteen or so tents. Well they used to be tents. Each one was flattened, torn to shreds and covered with blood and each one told the tale of what had happened here.

The people who owned these tents, the same people Conan the Barfuckingbarian had just annihilated, were obviously survivors who'd sheltered here on the island when the apocalypse started. How they'd contracted the virus was at that moment a mystery, but the domino effect that happened after each one had been infected was evident to see. It seems they'd all been sleeping when it happened and most had been attacked while inside their tents. The question was, why hadn't they sought shelter within the numerous buildings on the island?

Darren answered that when he went to investigate. 'They're all padlocked. Every one of them.'

He was right. Each padlock sat inside a thick metal box, so trying to lever them open or simply bash them with a hammer was impossible

'This lighthouse must be automated and controlled from somewhere else.' Darren added.

'Bollocks, how are we going to get in?' I asked. 'It's definitely not safe to sleep outside.'

Darren took off his backpack and produced a small leather pouch. Inside were thin strips of metal. I watched in awe as he deftly wiggled the metal inside of the padlock of a door of one of three buildings that looked to be cottages of some kind and with a click the padlock fell away from the lock.

'Darren mate, are you fucking kidding me?'

Darren just laughed, shrugged and opened the door.

Once upon a time this building had been the home of the lighthouse keeper and by the looks of the decor and furniture was vacated sometime in the eighties. Its lower floor consisted of a large living and dining room with an even larger kitchen at the rear of the property. The upper floor had two large double bedrooms and a family bathroom and had the same god-awful decor as downstairs. The furniture throughout was covered in sheets. It was dry, and once the wood-burning stoves were fired up would be warm too. Where we would get the wood from was another matter. If there was no fuel to be found, some of the furniture would do for now and then a sortie back to the mainland would probably be needed to source some fuel. This was a daunting prospect. Having just arrived at this safe haven the last thing I wanted to think about was going back there.

As Darren went back down to the beach to collect Andy, Bobby and the provisions from Andy's shop, I opened the metal lower floor shutters that covered the windows. I'd found the keys to their padlocks on the bench in the kitchen. The keys to the other buildings were nowhere to be found but I was sure inspector gadget would be able to open them if we needed to.

We decided not to put all our eggs in one basket, and split the food between the house and the boat. It took well over an hour to hump half of the of the food from the boat up to the house and another two to dump the deedaz that Darren destroyed into the sea and pile up all of the wrecked tents into a heap in an area behind the lighthouse. We planned on burning it later that night. We'd also found, in amongst the ruined campsite, some of the meagre provisions the islanders had owned. They were deemed unusable because most of it was covered in the gore of the slaughter that had occurred and the risk of contamination was too great and not worth the risk.

Amongst the tents we found the body of a deeda. It was in the latter stages of decomposition, bloated and practically green. This dead fuck was obviously the reason the small colony of survivors had been turned. The smelly green bastard must have been washed up onto the island in the night and attacked them while they slept. We wrapped him up in one of the broken tents and decided rather than carrying him back down to the sea we'd Guy Fawkes the fucker, and promptly threw him on the heap.

Darren reasoned that the night would disguise the smoke coming from the fire and the lighthouse would obscure any light from the flames being seen from the mainland. Advertising our whereabouts to other survivors or deedaz was deemed not a good idea at the present time.

> Securing our new home was now our number one priority.

Bobby went about storing and inventorying our supplies while Darren and I explored the other buildings.

The lighthouse and the building adjoining it actually did resemble a fortress. I later learned some of the history of the place from a book I found in one of the cottages.

The lighthouse was a 72-foot white square sandstone tower with walls more than one metre thick, surrounded by a turreted parapet. The adjoining white turreted building was a mystery to us. The padlock that held the large double doors shut was too corroded from the North Sea for us to enter but at a guess, looked like maybe it was a boat shed of some kind, that was used by the protection society that monitored the local bird population. The lighthouse, however, was accessible and we entered and climbed to the top to view the area.

Dusk was starting to set in, but from the vantage point we could see what was left of Amble on the mainland with the help of binoculars that we'd found on a desk. Numerous fires had had a disastrous effect on the harbour town, with most of the dead townsfolk standing in and around the ruins. Again, with nothing to stimulate them, they stood in stasis, endlessly waiting for something to bring them out of their trance and begin the hunt.

When the light was finally waning, Darren and I went back to the cottage to plan our next course of action.

On entering the cottage we were assaulted by the most tremendous aroma I'd ever experienced. A table had been set for the four of us and as we sat Bobby dished out huge helpings of what looked like corned beef hot pot with large chunks of potatoes and carrots.
It was the first real meal I'd had for what
seemed like a lifetime. I cried.

'Here he goes again,' said Darren.

'He's a right fucking puff.' 'Thanks

mate,' I sniffled.

After second helpings we all went and sat in the living room.

'Well?' I said to Darren.

Chapter 26 – The pirate

Darren told us his story. And what a story it was. Growing up on a farm had been hard for him and from an early age his father, who was in Greece on holiday when the zombies came, had instilled in him a strong work ethic. Maybe too strong. That and having next to no social life as a teenager drove Darren into the army when he came of age. After two years of excelling in the infantry Darren decided to put himself to the test and signed up for the special air service. Otherwise known as the SAS, it specialises in high-risk covert actions and similar anti-terrorism operations. There are four main troops that make up the SAS.

Boat troop, specialising in maritime skills.

Air troop, specialising in free-fall parachute insertion.

Mobility troop, specialists in using vehicles and experts in desert warfare.

Mountain troop, specialising in arctic combat and survival.

Darren, as it turned, out was part of mountain troop, and as well as possessing these skills was trained as a medic.

When his tour was up he joined R squadron. Its members all ex regular SAS regiment soldiers who committed to reserve service. At thirty-eight he left the service for good and returned home to the farm to help his ageing father with the running of it. That was two years ago, and now here he was on Coquet Island with a father and daughter and a sissy little cry baby who wets his pants every time he's scared.

It was getting late so Darren and I went to the lighthouse to burn what was left of the previous residents of the island. Darren produced a small petrol container and went to work dousing the wrecked tents with the fuel, giving the fisherman a double soaking. We stepped back as I struck one of the windproof matches from my survival kit and flicked it onto the mound. With a whoosh and a roar it went up. I stood and stared at the flames as they licked at the tents and fisherman, then turned towards where Darren should have been, but he wasn't. Shocked and panicked I turned 360 degrees in search of him. Nothing. He'd simply disappeared. WTF? Where was he? Had he been taken down by a deeda we'd missed? I'd surely have heard something if that was the case! My heart threatened to burst out of my chest. Alone again. I'd been lying to myself that I hadn't missed the company of my fellow man. I knew that having someone there to share this nightmare world with and to have them watch my back was the only way I could possibly endure this living hell. The past day since I met Darren had been the first time since all this happened that I'd had hope. Hope that I could survive this and regain some semblance of a life. Darren had survived because he was fearless, trained and had an unwavering confidence in himself. I'd survived by sheer fucking spawniness and I was sure my luck would run out sooner or later.

I took a deep breath and was about to shout his name when a hand covered my mouth from behind. I jumped, pulled away, turned and came face to face with a pirate. Yep, you heard me. A fucking pirate, patch and all I cowered and raised my hands and waited for his cutlass to strike me down.

'Calm down mate, it's me for fuck sake,' Darren hissed.

'Darren? Why the fucking hell are you dressed like a pirate?'

'It's only a patch on my eye Carter.' He replied. 'I put it on just before you threw the match on the bonfire. It stops the eye that's covered from losing its night vision from the light of the flames.'

'So where the fuck did you go?' I asked, trying my hardest not to show any fear in my voice.

'Well, once the fire was lit I went to the front of the light house to see if the fire could be seen. Sorry mate, I should have told you.'

'Yeah, you should have ye sneaky bastard,' I replied with a nudge of my elbow.

Darren snorted and we returned to staring at the fire.

After a couple of moments my heart calmed itself and then Darren started giggling like a schoolgirl.

'What?' I asked.

'Fucking pirate!' and with that we broke down in fits of laughter.

It's weird how the world can go to shit but the human being can still retain a sense of humour. Maybe it's the brain's way of keeping itself from snapping. After the past month living in this world of utter terror and death, the laughter we shared on that night really lifted my spirits. That and I wasn't alone again. I was lucky to have bumped into Darren. Very lucky. A total fucking killing machine when he needed to be. I had only known him a few hours and already, I knew, he would have my back and Andy's and Bobby's in any situation that arose. So what if it had just been luck that got me this far. I was still alive. That's all that counts in this new land.

After around an hour and not long after the giggling had stopped, the fire had burnt down to embers. The majority of the fisherman had been consumed by the fire but not all of it. With a shovel we'd found, we piled all of the embers onto the fisherman's remains and walked back to the house.

'There wasn't another boat when we arrived Darren,' I stated.

'Yeah, I was thinking that too mate,' he replied. 'How did they reach the island? The water is far too sketchy to swim across.'

I had no answer to that. We continued our walk back to the house in silence and deep in thought.

Chapter 27 – The shopkeeper

Once back I secured all of the window shutters and barred the front door from the inside in case any floaters happened to visit through the night.

Bobby boiled up some water in a huge pan and left the room while Darren, Andy and I stripped and scrubbed ourselves clean in the kitchen. The experience of washing with hot water and feeling clean threatened to tip me over the edge and start me weeping again. Luckily, I held it back. Crying in a room with two other naked men would probably get me evicted from the island. I definitely needed a chat with myself about keeping my emotions in check. Having the other survivors think that I was a weak link would not be good at all. I absolutely needed to up my game and to start making my own luck.

While Bobby took her turn to wash, the rest of us went into the living room wrapped in towels to discuss the sleeping arrangements.

Andy and Bobby took the main bedroom while I would bunk up with Darren in the smaller room.

Darren put together a rota for lookouts and we drew straws to see who'd get what. I drew the first watch and took my spot on the landing at the window, looking out over the front of the house and down to the jetty. It was decided that Bobby was exempt from this task as she had made the wonderful meal we ate. Also, I didn't really trust her to stay awake. The past few days of ferrying the provisions to the boat from their shop had noticeably taken its toll on the young lady. That and the constant fear of being eaten alive.

The night was divided up in to three shifts. Midnight till 2am, then the hardest watch of all, 2am till 4am, then the dawn watch from 4am till 6am. Andy drew the short straw and received the 2am till 4am slot with Darren taking the dawn watch.

Before everyone turned in for the night Andy told us their story of survival.

Again, as with me and Darren, Andy had seen the news broadcast on that fateful morning. He'd been up early waiting for the daily newspapers to be delivered. They never came. As soon as the news channels, media and communications systems shut down Andy jumped into action. Bobby and Andy lived in a flat above the business, which was only accessible through the shop or through the large garage/storage room at the back. The rollup garage door that led into the back lane behind the premises was reinforced and had a remote control for opening and closing. The shop front had shutters too, that could be controlled in the same way. So thirty seconds after learning of the upcoming apocalypse Andy and Bobby were as safe as anyone could be on the day humanity died. Andy had invested in solar panels years ago and with the fine weather he had been able to run the whole premises off the grid as soon as the main feed from the utilities supplier had been cut. With food and provisions to last them years they dug in and watched the end of days unfold. Bobby excused herself at this point and went to bed, obviously not wanting to relive the terrible things she had seen.

    Andy continued. The next few days had been dark days indeed. From their vantage point looking over the main road that ran through Stakeford they watched it all unfold. The first deeda they saw was a young girl of fourteen. He knew her age because he knew the girl. She'd come in for her weekly horse riding magazine. She'd been terrible bitten on both arms, injuries obviously received while trying to fight off whoever bit her. Bobby had insisted that they go down and help the girl. She hadn't seen the news flash so didn't really understand what was going on. She finally came to terms with the situation when the poor girl with the bitten arms attacked a middle-aged woman who'd stopped her car to help. Before she could get her seatbelt off the young deeda had launched herself through the open car window and attacked. Stories like this happened again and again but after a few days the killing stopped and all that remained were the walking dead.

It was three weeks later that Andy made the decision to leave. He'd seen sporadic fires breaking out through the area and knew it was just a matter of time before they made it to the shop.

As soon as this mess started he'd had the boatyard plan in the back of his mind. His friend had a boat stored there and Andy had been there countless times while fishing.

With the pickup truck loaded with food, Andy and Bobby struck out to check that an escape by boat would be possible. Andy had checked the back lane for deedaz before he opened the garage door from the safety of the pickup.

As soon as they were clear he closed it again with the remote. The back lane was surprisingly free of deedaz but at the end of the road a gaggle of them had started to enter, curious as to the noise the truck made. Now, the pickup they were driving was a high-end one. Not one of these beat-up cowboy things. This was the cream of the cream. A Toyota Hilux with heightened suspension and a bull bar on the front that could knock buildings down. It had a single cab and an enclosed bed for supplies. The last thing Andy wanted to do was damage his baby, so he simply ploughed slowly through the nosey deedaz. A couple of them were knocked over and crushed under the large heavy tyres. The rest banged futilely on the windows as the vehicle glided by. Being only three and a half miles away and travelling on a back road that was rarely used, they arrived after around ten minutes.

The boatyard was locked up tight, which was a good sign. Andy bent down and from under a large black rock produced the key for the padlock holding the gates together. After emptying the provisions into the shipping container and checking that Andy's friend's boat was in ship shape, they locked everything up tight and left, taking the key for the padlock with a them. When they got back to the shop, Andy slowly drove the truck up the back lane. The deedaz that were there followed. When he got to the end he floored it to the left and then left again and made it back to the garage door having left the stupid deedaz behind. With a click of the remote the garage opened and the truck slipped in. Andy and Bobby repeated this around fifteen times during the next couple of weeks. Always succeeding but having had some very close shaves indeed. His story ended at the part when two strange men came tootling along the lane in a John Deere.

When everyone went to bed I took a chair and went and sat on the upstairs landing. From my position I had an unobstructed view through the window of the approach to the island and the beach and jetty.

My shift went without any drama and my thoughts again turned to my ex's safety. I couldn't shake the feeling that she needed me somehow, but getting to her from the island would have been an impossible task. Plus, there was a strong chance she'd fled to somewhere safer or, heaven forbid, become a walking corpse. I knew if the latter was true I'd have probably given up on surviving and walked into her arms for one final cuddle.

The feelings of guilt weighed heavy on me for not taking the detour to see if she was safe. Though, If I had gone, I wouldn't be on the island, I'd never have met Darren and I'd have never gotten through Cambois without that tractor.

Andy relieved me at 2am and with a heavy heart I went to bed expecting again to be haunted in my dreams. After the weeks I'd spent sleeping on the hard floorboards of the loft, the feeling of jumping into a real bed was amazing. I kept the sobbing to a minimum, but the bed and the fact I felt relatively safe with someone watching over me was something I had never expected to feel again.

Chapter 28 – The padlock

I awoke to the bright sun shining through the grimy bedroom window, the amazing aroma of breakfast being cooked and the sound of the creaking shutters of the windows on the ground floor being opened. After quickly changing into the clean clothes from my bugout bag and finally getting out of that fucking onesie, I descended the stairs and found everyone in the kitchen. Clean clothes were sported by all. More noticeably, Darren was decked out in full army combat regalia looking every inch the soldier he was.

Andy told me to sit and then proceeded to dish out a veritable feast. Powdered eggs, beans, fried spam, tinned mushrooms and tinned tomatoes. We talked while we ate as if it were just an ordinary day and the terrors of the world hadn't happened. That feeling came to an end when Darren said that we needed a plan of action for the day ahead. If it was up to me we'd have a day off. After the past few weeks, I just wanted to relax and soak up the feeling of safety the island gave. Darren, however, was one of those people who always needed a purpose. Something to conquer. A mission to undertake. He was the leader now.

Who was I to argue?

It was decided that a lookout was needed 24/7 and should be positioned up in the lighthouse during daylight hours and in the house during the night. Andy volunteered to take the watch for the day while Darren and I opened the rest of the buildings that were locked around the island. Bobby was tasked with getting the house sorted by removing the furniture coverings and generally making the place liveable. She'd be alone, but having Andy watching our backs and hers we knew she'd be as safe as she was ever going to be.

Before Darren and I left to explore I strapped on my machete and hatchet and went to pick up my crossbow.

'Just leave that mate,' Darren said as he opened one side of his jacket. There, in a chest holster, was some sort of pistol. With a Darren grin he said, 'Say hello to my leetle friend'.

Apart from Andy's 'shotgun' and the helicopter gun, this was the first time I'd seen a real gun up close. Apparently it was a Glock 17, 17 being the number of 9mm rounds it held. I wasn't sure whether I felt safer or not. As I'd mentioned earlier, guns were not a common thing in the UK. In fact it felt totally alien to me to be this close to one. I knew that Darren had been trained to use such a thing but the fear was if it fell into the wrong hands. I mentioned this to Darren to which he replied, 'The only way this gun will be taken from me is from my cold dead hands, and if that happens Carter, you're proper fucked'.

With that sobering thought hanging in the air he turned and went outside. I followed like a lost puppy not wanting to be far from the protective field that positively surrounded Darren. I knew if there was any chance of surviving the ZA it would happen only if I was in close proximity to him.

We decided to open the locks on the other two houses. The first one seemed to be an exact replica of the house we'd claimed. The second, however, had some sort of workshop in the living room. The dining room had been repurposed into a storeroom for fuel with sacks upon sacks of smokeless coal, logs and kindling. Thankfully, a journey back to the mainland wouldn't be needed now for quite some time.

Upstairs we found a room full of waterproof clothing of different sizes and a room full of scuba diving equipment. The reason for this equipment being there was lost on us. At a guess it was owned by the marine/wildlife researchers that once used the island.

Darren started searching amongst the shelves and cupboards in the tool room and eventually found what he was looking for. 'Aha!' he exclaimed. In his hand was a can of WD40 lubricating oil. I had no idea what on earth he planned to do with it.

'Follow me bonny lad,' he cheerfully said and led me out of the house and towards the large padlocked building adjoined to the lighthouse. On arriving he went to work with the WD40 on the keyhole of the padlock. I doubted he would get the prehistoric looking security device open. After five minutes of waiting he produced his lock picks from one of his many pockets and attacked the lock.

As I was watching him I noticed grooves in the ground in front of the building which were obviously made by the out-swinging doors. I also noticed that the grooves seemed relatively fresh. How could that be? That lock hadn't been opened in years judging by the rust and the difficulty Darren was having in opening it. I stood back to get a better look. The chain that the padlock was attached to passed through holes in each of the large metal doors. Then it dawned on me why the locks were so old and unused.

'Darren?' I said.

'Yeah mate?' He replied.

'If I can get that door open in less than five seconds, will you teach me how to use that gun?' I asked.

'Ha, if you can do it in less than an hour I'll teach you how to use it and give you my spare gun.'

'WTF mate, you've got another gun?' I asked.

'Did you just say 'WTF' instead of what the fuck?' he asked laughingly.

'Never mind that, have you another gun?' I asked again.

'No mate, I've another three!' he proclaimed.

Speechless and shaking my head I walked towards the doors and put my hand into one of the holes the chain went through. I followed the chain down to the nail that the end was looped onto and unhooked it, pulled it through and triumphantly showed it to Darren. The lock and chain were only there for effect. Most likely so whatever was held inside the building could be accessed easily and without the fuss of having to look for the key.

It had probably fooled just about everyone who'd seen it. Including Darren.

All he could say was 'WTF'.

At this we both turned back into the giggling schoolgirls until tears streamed down our faces. I've had giggle attacks before, stoned ones, church ones and bingo ones, but apocalypse ones have got to be the most rewarding giggles you can get. All that pent-up fear, mixed with the relief at being alive must cause the mind to behave differently. I only just made it to the corner of the building to relieve myself. After all the pissy pants I'd experienced since the start of ZA, I never thought I'd be pissing myself with laughter, when just two days previously, I'd been contemplating suicide in the loft.

Once the giggles had passed and Andy had shouted down from the lighthouse to 'knock it the fuck off', we entered the large doorway. Directly inside the door was a small tractor. I say tractor; it was more like a sit-on lawn mower to be honest. Behind it, on a trailer, was a zodiac with a large 120hp outboard motor. A zodiac is a boat. It has a solid bottom and a large inflatable tube that encircles the rigid hull. In the centre of the hull towards the back is a console with a steering wheel and throttle lever. My mate used to have more or less the same type with only a 90hp outboard on, but boy could it move.

We used to take it across to the Lake District in the summer and camp out, smoke weed, take pills, and play and sing songs with the aid of my acoustic guitar, which usually ended up with us being thrown off the site at an ungodly hour when the singing got too rambunctious.

The last time we went we were thrown off approximately one hour after we arrived. We hadn't even set the tents up. Someone thought it a good idea to take the boat for a spin on the lake first and then thought it a good idea to produce some ready rolled spliffs. Half an hour later the four of us were stoned immaculate and carelessly drifting towards the Ullswater boating club.

Now a whitey is a condition many stoners know all too well. The unavoidable spinning sensation is usually followed by projectile vomiting. This ailment is always brought on by smoking too much weed or mixing the leaf with alcohol. Well the whitey that struck my friend Paul was a seasickness whitey. A force ten on the whitey scale.

So imagine the looks of disgust we got from the guests at the boating club's annual summer fete when Paul went off like old faithful. The geyser that spewed hot stomach acid into the air and down on to our little boat set of a whitey chain reaction, and before we knew it we looked like the Bellagio fountain show in Las Vegas.

Needless to say, the owner of the campsite was informed of our behaviour, expelled us forth with and barred us for life.

Chapter 29 – The questions

Back in the garage where the tractor and zodiac were, Darren turned the ignition key on the small tractor. It started first time. I told Darren I thought we should use this boat if we ever needed to get to the mainland for any reason. It was much lighter than the fishing boat we'd used to get to the island and we could beach it and re-float it without much effort. It was also as fast as hell.

Darren agreed and we planned to move it down to the beach the next day. After cutting the tractor engine we suddenly heard whistling coming from outside. As we ran out,

Andy shouted down. 'Ship!'

Darren and I bounded up the lighthouse stairs to where Andy was situated. Directly to the east on the horizon was a ship.

Darren took the binoculars off Andy and told him to keep watch to the western approach to the island. After looking he held the binos out for me to use.

'It's a Royal Navy destroyer,' he said.

My heart leapt. I grabbed the binoculars and quickly zeroed in on the boat. It was large and grey with what looked like a tall thin pyramid in its centre with a large ball on top.

Could this be our salvation? Could it be over? Were they looking for survivors? My jubilations were short lived when I glanced at Darren.

'What's wrong?' I asked.

'Aren't we going to signal them?' Darren sat deep in thought for a good while.

'So?' I asked again.

Darren, as it happens is even more paranoid than me and is of the thinking if something is too good to be true it usually is. On his watch the previous night, he'd spent his time wisely and had been scanning the radio channels, military and civilian, looking for fellow survivors. He'd heard nothing. He surmised that if this ship was indeed looking for survivors, we surely would have received a broadcast of some kind in advance of it arriving. As I was listening to Darren's reasoning I happened to spot a small fishing vessel travelling on a southeast heading on a direct course with the ship. The boat must have come from one of the small harbours to the north of us.

The ship had obviously spotted it too and slowed to a stop. Within forty-five minutes the small fishing vessel had arrived at its destination and Darren gave a running commentary of what was happening as he looked through the binoculars.

'They seem to be talking to each other with bullhorns. The man on the fishing vessel looks to be taking his clothes off. He's got his hands in the air. This doesn't look good guys.
Ah, fuck.'

Darren lowered the binoculars just as the sound wave of a high-powered chain machine gun hit us. I put the binoculars to my eyes just in time to see the fishing vessel disappear beneath the rolling waves. I slowly sat down in the chair behind me.

'What the fuck is going on?' Andy asked.

'They blew him out of the fucking water,' I replied.

Darren's face was blank. Why did they kill him? was my first question. Fuck me. What if we'd signalled them? was my second.

Darren came out of his daydream and suggested possible scenarios of what had happened. His first, was that the man in the fishing boat was infected and they'd seen this when he'd stripped his clothes off. This couldn't be right though. The infected usually turned in a matter of seconds. Unless something had changed in the infection process.

His second scenario was that the sailors on board the destroyer weren't loyal to her majesty anymore and had turned into pirates, shooting down the naked man when he'd confessed to having nothing of value.

The third scenario, and this was the bitter sweet one, was that the UK was a quarantine zone. This meant the rest of the world was uninfected, which was really good news but meant the British people were on their own and the chances of getting away from this place with a patrolling navy destroyer were slim to none.

We decided not to signal the murdering fucks and planned to cover all windows of the house to blot out any light in case the patrol passed during the night and clocked us.

With our spirits dampened we returned to the house for some lunch and promised to send some up for Andy as soon as we were done.

Bobby was to be kept in the dark regarding the ship incident. She'd asked what the noise was but we palmed her off by saying it was a building collapsing in Amble. She'd been through enough lately and she didn't need to have another thing to worry about.

After lunch Darren disappeared upstairs and I took Andy his lunch and stayed with him for a while. I told him about the decision we took about not telling Bobby about the occurrences of the morning and he agreed, thanking us for being so thoughtful.

I returned to the house and entered the living room. Darren was there sitting on the chair next to the fireplace. Before him on the floor lay what can only be described as an arsenal. Guns, grenades, scopes, what looked like a man-shaped bush, tins of camouflage paint, knives of different sizes, medikit and four black boxes with two prongs sticking from the bottom of each of them.

> The events that took place before lunch looked to have spurred Darren into action.
>
> 'What's happening mate?' I asked.
>
> 'Not a lot Carter mate, just need to get my shit sorted and stick to the six p's: proper preparation

prevents piss poor performance. This island needs securing. We can't trust anyone.'

Now I for one did not like this line of thinking. The only people I'd met since the shit hit the fan were just normal people. Well, apart from Darren that is. We couldn't start tarring everyone with the same brush. What sort of world would that be? We definitely couldn't turn people away if they needed help. I reiterated my thoughts to Darren and thankfully he understood where I was coming from. He changed his statement to, 'we must be cautious with everyone'.

We went about securing the beach first. Darren said if someone were to come and bring harm to us they'd do it stealthily, and with the beach being the only real access to the island they'd come ashore there. Anyone with ill intentions would then skirt around the coast of the island on either side and attack from the rear. With this said he took out one of the boxes with the prongs on and stuck it in the ground on the left side of the beach where sand met soil. He repeated this on the right side. The claymore mines he'd just set had a proximity sensor which was sensitive to around five feet. Once triggered it would explode, sending hundreds of ball bearings in the direction it was pointed at. We then decided to take the rest of the provisions from the boat and store them in the other unoccupied house, leaving a month's supply in the boat in case we had to make a sharp exit.

Darren then went about booby trapping the boat in case it was stolen. One of Darren's ten grenades was tasked to this purpose. If anyone tried to move the large rock the mooring line was under the grenade would go off. This shouldn't damage the boat but would damage any light fingers in the vicinity.

After warning Andy and Bobby of the new dangers on the island, Darren took me to the rear of the lighthouse and proceeded to teach me the correct procedures for handling firearms. Before I got to hold the Glock I had to learn how to clean it. Then the loading of the weapon and finally the correct way to hold it. After two hours of intense training I finally held it in my hands.

'Can I shoot it now?' I asked excitedly.

'I think your ready matey,' replied Darren.

Darren told me to aim for a large rock that was sitting precariously on the top of the easterly cliff.

With gun pointed down I disengaged the safety, brought the pistol up, aimed, squeezed the trigger gently, exhaled and fired. The heavy recoil and loud bang I expected never came.

'Have I broken it?'

He hadn't even fucking loaded it. Apparently bullets are worth more than gold now and the chance of attracting attention with the subsequent noise was deemed too great. I reluctantly agreed he was right and tried my hardest not to show how disappointed I was. 'You're not gonna fucking cry again are you?' he jokingly asked. 'Don't worry mate, I've got something cool to show you tonight,' he added.

Chapter 30 – The apparition

Dinner was ready when we arrived back at the house. I quickly wolfed down the tinned chilli con carne and went up to the lighthouse to relieve Andy. He'd been solid today, never once taking his eyes from his surroundings, but judging by his face he was done in. I found out later he didn't even eat, he just went straight to bed.

As the sun went down visibility decreased drastically so I went down to the house to keep an eye on the beach from the landing window. I'd asked Darren to help me take one of the comfortable chairs up to sit on while on watch. He told me to do so would be a bad idea. The more comfortable you are the more likely you are to fall asleep. Again I reluctantly agreed and headed up to the uncomfortable wooden dining chair. Bobby took Andy's shift that night.

Thirty minutes into my watch Darren appeared at my side like a ghost and put the shits right up me.

'Fuckin' hell mate, will you please stop doing that?' I begged.

'Ha, sorry mate, I don't know I'm doing it. Force of habit. Here.'

He handed me a short tube. It was a night sight with infrared capabilities.

'That'll keep you busy,' he said. 'Just use the night vision mainly; the IR won't pick up any of the stinkaz with them being dead and all. Don't worry about the batteries, I've a shit load of them.'

I looked through the sights. A green hue covered everything in view. I could see as clear as day all the way down to the boat on the beach.

'This is fucking awesome Darren, how the fuck does it work? Gotta be magic.' I took my eyes from the reticule to see why he wasn't answering and he was gone. For fuck's sake.

At midnight one of the most bizarre things I've ever seen happened. The novelty of the night scope had worn off an hour earlier so I'd started to use it sparingly every ten minutes or so. As I was about to take another look through it something caught my eye from the south. At first I thought I was seeing things, that I'd damaged my eyes somehow with overuse of the scope. A rainbow of bright lights seemed to be travelling toward the gap between the island and the mainland. I sat there for a minute or two trying to fathom what on earth I was seeing in the distance. It was like some luminescent deep-sea creature that undulated and throbbed with pulsating multi-coloured light. It couldn't be that though. This was far away and would have to be huge to catch my eye from such a distance. Eventually my mind remembered the military-grade scope I was holding. I turned off the night vision and brought the scope to my eye.

It was a boat. Travelling under its own steam. The lights I could see were disco lights and it looked as though there was some sort of party going on. WTF? Did they know something we didn't? Had the zompoc been quashed in the past twenty-four hours? Could something have made all the zombies drop down dead? Well, drop down deader? Were the survivors of the initial cull now celebrating the demise of the zombie plague.

I'd felt this way earlier in the day when I thought salvation was just a destroyer ship away. I felt hope. Hope can be a good thing to have. It can get you through the darkest times and can spur you on to do things you never thought you could. But to have it ripped away time and again can start to have the opposite effect and can breed pessimism, which is only a small step away from despair.

I chose not to alert Darren, Andy and Bobby from their slumber. I needed to ascertain first whether or not the disco boat was a threat to us.

It took fifteen minutes for the boat to get close enough for me to see the passengers clearly. Despair was beginning to rear its ugly head.

The boat was full, full of the dead.

Unbelievingly, I actually recognised the boat, having sailed on it numerous times over the years. It was the Tyne Party Ferry. On weekdays it would carry passengers back and forth across the Tyne river; at weekends it would become a floating hen/stag party venue selling cheap booze and playing loud music.

Leaving the quayside of Newcastle at 7pm, it would traverse easterly towards Tynemouth, perform a u-turn at the coast and head back. This usually took around four hours and by this time the revellers on the boat were either comatose or shouting for Huey over the gun whales of the boat.

I'd never been a passenger on said party nights. I'd been the live entertainment on the many times I'd sailed on her. I'd had some wild nights on that boat and some fond memories. To be seeing it now on the open sea with its disco lights flashing and its passengers dancing to the zombie bop was surreal to say the least. I wracked my brains to think of a scenario of what happened on its ill-fated voyage. How did the people turn? How had it gotten so far up the coast under its own steam? How was it not shipwrecked or beached? Why were the fucking disco lights on?

As it got closer to the island it suddenly changed course. No way. Was there someone alive on there? There couldn't be. There had to be at least fifty to sixty dead on board.

I focused the scope on the wheelhouse which was situated on top of the boat's main central room. There, in vivid technicolour, was the ship's captain. He was alive but wouldn't be for long. He'd obviously been steering the boat along the coast for some reason. Where he was going was anyone's guess.

The change of course was brought on by numerous deedaz trying to push their way into the wheel house. The captain, realising the steering of the boat was no longer a priority and the barring of the door was, let go of the wheel and threw himself up against the door. He soon tired and the door slowly started to inch its way open. Strangely, the last action of the captain was to lunge for the steering console and press a button of some kind. The door burst open followed by the deedaz. The end was swift for the unlucky sailor.

The button he'd pressed must have been some sort of auto pilot feature because the boat powered on, straight and true, out to the open sea.

'Fucking hell,' was whispered in my ear.

I screamed like a girl. 'For god's sake Darren, will you stop fucking doing that. Honestly mate, my family history is riddled with heart disease. Mine isn't going to last much longer with you doing that shit!'

Darren laughed. 'Just trying to toughen you up mate. You'll stop getting shocked sooner or later. I'm training you and you don't even know it,' he added.

Then in his best batman voice he said, 'Come on Robyn, to the lighthouse!'

Before we left I gently whispered into Andy and Bobby's room that someone needed to watch the beach. Andy was up in a flash, obviously the early night had recharged his batteries somewhat.

'What's going on?' he asked.

Darren told him not to worry and that we would be back shortly.

Within minutes we were there. From the commanding view the lighthouse gave we could see the ghost boat, about a mile out, still powering through the waves and still on the same course.

'Get ready for the fireworks,' Darren proclaimed.

Fireworks? What was he on about? Then, as if on cue, a bright white light from the southern horizon flared and launched straight into the sky. In an almost lethargic way it slowly arced towards the ghost ship. The sky lit up as the ferry exploded into a million bits. The explosion was well over a mile away but within seconds the heat from it could be felt on our exposed skin. Fucking hell.

Again, I looked at Darren for answers and again he was in deep thought.

'It still doesn't tell us a fucking thing,' he announced after five minutes.

'We still have the three scenarios Carter and we're no closer to resolving which scenario we're in.'

After standing there in silence for another five minutes pondering what our futures held we headed back to the house and informed Andy of the latest developments while Bobby was upstairs keeping watch. The next hour was spent discussing our next move.

Darren deduced that the destroyer either had to have some type of drone chaperoning the ship, which had confirmed the ferry was occupied by the dead. Or that the destroyer was just using its radar and blowing the shit out of anything approaching the 'quarantine' buffer zone.

Either way we decided that our presence on the island must be camouflaged as much as possible from now on. The fishing boat would be swapped with the zodiac as soon as possible and be stored in the large building. The zodiac would be situated on the grass next to the beach and promptly covered with something to make it invisible from the air and mainland.

With a plan of action for the following day we retired for the night.

As I lay there trying to sleep I did my nightly replay of the day's events. It seemed good news was always followed with bad. We'd found the awesome stash of fuel, tools and zodiac and then witnessed the harrowing murder of the naked sailor which in turn created so many unanswerable questions. Questions that soon had my tired mind drifting off to sleep. True to form my last thought was of her. The ex. With every day that passed her chances of being alive grew smaller. I knew in my heart of hearts that she most definitely had been killed or turned in the early days, but there is always hope. I would continue to hope until I was presented with proof to contradict it.

Chapter 31 – The shape of things to come

By all accounts Bobby's shift went without drama, no ghost ships or Exocet missiles were seen at all. Darren's, however, didn't. At 5:30am I was roughly shaken awake by Darren.

'We've got company,' he proclaimed.

Usually it takes me around three or four snoozes of my alarm to get up. Not anymore. I woke, refreshed and surprised again at having another dreamless sleep. I quickly got dressed in my day-old bugout clothes and was ready for action in minutes. My mind raced. Could the navy have found us? Had they spotted us the day before? Had they sent a death squad to exterminate us?

I looked out of the window and was surprised when I saw a sailing boat angling its way to our jetty.

Turning around to ask Darren what we should do next, I was surprised to see that he'd vanished into thin air. Again. Fuckin sneaky bastard!

By the time I'd laced up my shoes, fastened my weapon belt and exited the front door the people in the boat had disembarked and were walking toward the lighthouse. There were three of them.

'Hello there,' I shouted.

'This is my island,' one of them said as they approached. He was a large man around thirty years old, bristling with menace and covered in tattoos. He was also carrying a rifle with a scope on it. How has everyone got a fucking gun? His accomplices, I would guess, we're in their late teens or early twenties.

Foolishly I said, 'Ah, so you must be the Duke of Northumberland. Pleased to meet you.' I'd learned this information on the day we arrived, from a pamphlet I'd found in the kitchen.

'Funny fucker aren't you?' he said.

'Haway mate, there's plenty of room on this island to share, it's safe from the zombies and I don't take up much room.' I didn't mention the fact that I wasn't alone. He hadn't asked so wasn't about to show my hand. I especially wasn't going to tell him that we had in our company a pretty eighteen-year-old girl.

'Where the fuck are our people that were camped here? And what the fuck caused that explosion through the night?' He asked.

'Mate, I just arrived the day before yesterday and they were all zombies. One of them must have washed up on to the island and attacked your friends through the night. I haven't a clue what the explosion was. It scared the shit out of me,' I lied.

'They weren't friends of ours, they paid us to live here. They gave us shit and we didn't kill them, that was the deal. Now all we have is you. Got any food?' he asked.

'A little,' I lied

'Well that ours now. You've got five minutes to jump in your boat and fuck off or I'm going to finish you'

Now that his intentions were clear I weighed up my situation. There I was, alone and being threatened by three men. Well, one man. The other two looked like they weren't enjoying their new vocation into piracy very much at all.

I decided to play along with their leader for a while longer and knew that Darren was around somewhere. I hoped.

'Can I at least take my bag with me?' I asked.

'Just hurry the fuck up and show me the food first,' he ordered.

I walked up to the cottage and was followed inside by tattoo boy.

'How did you get in to the house?' he asked.

'I found the keys on a hook next to the back door,' I lied again.

'Gippa is going to fuckin love this,' he muttered.

I presumed Gippa was a friend of tattoo boy's and gathered Gippa would most probably be the new owner of the house very soon if tattoo boy had anything to do with it. It was a name that seemed fleetingly familiar to me for some reason. I discarded the thought as quickly as it entered my head. My life was in peril and I was absolutely under no illusions that my days were numbered as soon as he saw and stole our supplies.

'Stay outside and keep fuckin watch,' he said to the other two.

He obviously wanted first choice on the food we had. Looking at his accomplices it had been this way for a long time. Judging by their appearance they hadn't been eating very well at all, whereas tattoo boy gave the appearance of having seven square meals a day.

I took him through the house and into the dining room where the food was stored. His eyes grew to the size of saucers when he laid them on our provisions.

'Wh... wh... what the fuck?' Was all he could muster.
I used to have a book on my bedside table at home. It was called 'Famous last words'. In it, was a collection of final utterances from people throughout history. Kings, celebrities, poets, painters, actors, musicians. If I ever get home to that book I'm going to make sure I add tattoo boy's final words into it.

'Wh... Wh.... What the fuck!' Haha. Classic.

Darren stood there, over the prone form of tattoo boy, looking down at him with a crazed bloodlust in his eyes. I was a little wary of him at first, but like the flicking of a switch his face changed and he was back to good old grinning Darren.

'What the fuck Darren?'

'Ha, that's what he said,' was Darren's reply.

'Where are the other two?' I asked.

'Knocked the fuckers out.' And with that he turned and left the room the way he came in. I stepped over tattoo boy and followed, trying not to look at the very large dent in the back of his head and the pool of blood collecting on the dining room floor.

Outside, Darren was in the process of hog tying dead tattoo boy's accomplices.

Andy and Bobby decided to make an appearance and again asked, 'What the fuck?'

After explaining what had happened to Andy and Bobby, Darren none too gently slapped the remaining 'pirates' awake and began to interrogate them. He'd obviously had some sort of training in this practice because before too long they started singing like fucking canaries. In fact, I'm sure if Darren had told them to, they would have.

The most talkative of the two was called Josh, the other Damien. He told us the exislanders were practically prisoners on the island. Tattoo boy and his 'friends' had taken the numerous boats that had brought the now dead residents to the rock and effectively trapped them all. This rendered them unable to escape when the seemingly impregnable wall of sea had been breached by the dead.

We learned that they were part of a larger group of around thirty people, mostly men, who were holed up in a large old warehouse on the outskirts of Amble. Inside they'd set up a kind of tent city. Apparently the building had a large courtyard and both were surrounded by a large wall. A large garage in the corner of the courtyard had in it enough food to last them months.

We also learned they were dangerous and offered 'protection' to other small groups in the locality. They took from them whatever they wanted. Clothes, water, food, flesh. 'So you're fucking rapists?' Darren fumed.

'No,' they answered in unison. 'We were holed up in the yacht club building with our families before they came. They killed our parents and took us to the compound around a week ago. They keep us and a few others locked in a shed until they need us. We're used to ferry them around in the sail boats or to take them fishing.'

They told us there was a pecking order in this new draconian society. The biggest and meanest of them had first pickings on food and women.

I turned and looked at Darren. His face a mask of fury and revenge!

Darren had a new mission!

To be continued...

30610282R00106

Printed in Poland
by Amazon Fulfillment
Poland Sp. z o.o., Wrocław